FIRST LINE DEFENSE

A novel by

Thomas E. Krupowicz

TERK BOOKS AND PUBLISHERS

Chicago, Illinois

Copyright 1995 by Thomas E. Krupowicz
All Rights Reserved
Printed in the United States of America

This novel is entirely a work of fiction. Names, characters, places, times and incidents are either the product of the author's imagination or are used fictitiously. Any resemblance to actual events or places or persons, living or dead, is entirely coincidental.

No part of this book may be reproduced or transmitted in any form by any means, electronic or mechanical, including photography, recording, or any information storage or retrieval system, without permission in writing from the author.

Cover illustration by **Steven Krupowicz**

ISBN: **1-881690-02-4**

TERK BOOKS & PUBLISHERS
P.O. BOX 160
PALOS HEIGHTS, ILLINOIS 60463

This novel is dedicated to a very special person -- MOM -- who loves to read police stories and watch police programs on TV.

Other books published by **TERK BOOKS & PUBLISHERS**

DEATH DANCED AT THE BOULEVARD BALLROOM
by   Thomas E. Krupowicz
ISBN: 1-881690-00-8
12.95

FINGERPRINTS--THE IDENTITY FACTORS
by   Thomas E. Krupowicz
ISBN: 1-881690-01-6
39.95

CHAPTER 1

"All new recruits report to rooms 101 and 102!" barked a rough, gravel like masculine voice from the large black speakers hanging from the ceiling, at each end of the long hallway.

Ted Namsky put out his cigarette in the sand filled metal container. He followed the long hallway, along with other new recruits, looking stupidly for the wooden doors marked 101 and 102.

An overstuffed middle-aged man, wearing sergeant's chevrons on the sleeve of his police uniform shirt, stood in a doorway and greeted the men who were assigned to room 101.

"Take any one of those seats and make yourselves comfortable," he said roughly, then smiled pleasantly. Suddenly, the long hallway echoed with the deafening sounds of buzzers and bells.

"That's the signal for changing classrooms!" barked the sergeant, losing all of his pleasantness after the men were seated. "You men," he continued, "will be together until the day that you graduate from this Academy. Before we go any further, I suggest that we introduce ourselves and maybe give a little explanation of our previous occupation."

Each man turned and introduced himself to the man sitting on either side of him. Within minutes, the classroom was filled with the voices of fifty people.

The sergeant, his face starting to redden because of the commotion that had started, stood in front of the classroom, clearing his throat loudly, trying to get some attention! Finally, his voice towered loudly over everyone else's. "Hey! You fuckin' clods. Quiet!" he shouted. Instant silence prevailed throughout the classroom. The sergeant rested his buttocks on the edge of his desk. "Sergeant O'Ryan's my name," he smiled, "and getting you assholes ready for the street is the name of this game!"

A feeling of relief overtook everyone, upon seeing a smile beginning to form on the sergeant's lips. This was the sergeant's standard opening speech each time he greeted a new batch of police recruits. A few strands of his salt-and- pepper color curly hair hung down onto his forehead as his eyes slowly surveyed the men sitting before him.

"We're waiting for the lieutenant to swear you all in as police officers," he said. He picked up a clipboard from off the top of his desk. "But, in the meantime," he paused, "let me take roll call to see if everyone's accounted for." At the conclusion of the roll call, the classroom door opened. A neatly dressed, six-foot-three inch, dark curly haired man entered the classroom.

"Good morning,, Lieutenant," blurted out Sergeant O'Ryan. The lieutenant smiled, replying, "Good morning, Sergeant!" He turned and faced the recruits.

"Men," he paused, "I'm Lieutenant James Kleeman, from the Recruit Processing Section. I'm here to swear you all in as police officers. If you will all please stand up and raise your right hand, I'll administer the oath of your office for you."

At the conclusion of giving the oath, the recruits sat down and began to fill out an endless sea of forms that never seemed to stop coming - pension fund papers; death beneficiary forms; hospitalization forms; etc., etc.

The signal bell for the first lunch hour finally gave its call. Ted Namsky was grateful that it had. His right index finger was numb from all the writing. His finger felt as though there was a six-foot gully running down the center of it.

Ted wandered from room to room, searching for that small lunchroom that was supposed to be hidden somewhere in the building. At last he was successful. He had completed his first assignment!

Upon entering the drab colored room, the first thing that caught his eye were the vending machines, neatly lined up against the wall. He visualized them to be tall, majestic slot machines, just standing there, coaxing the people to come over and try their luck. The line in front of each machine held at least twenty hungry and thirsty recruits.

Ted decided that he wasn't really hungry after all. A walk would really be much better right now. Besides, he hadn't had a chance to completely check the building over. Before he had decided to come to the Academy, a friend had told him that the Academy was over a hundred years old. A city as big as this, having an outdated building for a Police Academy, this Ted Namsky found hard to believe. Now that he was inside the building, he believed his friend's story.

The ceilings and walls had been patched repeatedly. Besides squeaking loudly, the floor boards seemed to shift with each step that one took.

Ah, tradition! thought Ted. That's why they still use this old building! A great thing, this tradition!...

CHAPTER II

The first weeks past quickly. Their studies consisted of introductions into difficult subjects and indoctrination into many practices. Logic, mental and reasoning tests also filled that entire week's schedule.

Ted Namsky's second week at the Academy was a little more interesting. He received his first introduction into the *FATMAN CLUB*. This elite club consisted not only of men who were a little plump around the midsection, but also *MISFITS* who could not complete the required amount of push-ups, sit-ups and chin-ups. The club was run entirely on the merit system. Instead of eating lunch, one ate *SWEAT!* These specially chosen men of the elite club would devote all of their lunch time to doing exercises.

Ted's hang-up was the chinning bar. He couldn't master the art of chinning himself. No matter how hard he tried. Every time he reached his sixth chin-up, his wrists would feel as if all his power was slowly seeping away and he would fall to the ground.

On the first day's encounter with the *FATMAN'S CLUB* Ted was surprised to see that there was standing room only. The first person to catch Ted's attention was short and stocky. The recruit was letting his hands rest comfortably against the wall. He leaned forward. Just before his chin would touch the wall, he would push himself away from the wall.

Ted walked over to the recruit and asked about the type of exercise he was supposed to be doing. "*PUSH-UPS, STUPID! PUSH-UPS!*" the reply came back.

Another member of the club stood on a chair under a chinning bar. He'd bend down and then gradually pull his chin over the bar. If he would have stood erect on the chair, his chest would have been even with the chinning bar!

Ted laughed silently to himself and shook his head from side to side as he searched for a spot to do his exercises.

CHAPTER III

It only took a few days for the new recruits to find special friends. Ted Namsky had chosen Tim Barner and Leon Bukowski.

Monday morning was always examination day. The recruits sat nervously at their desks, trying to memorize the notes from the past week's lectures. If your total average marks fell below seventy, there was a good chance that you would be dropped from the Academy.

The handwritten notes taken by the recruits from the previous week's lectures had to be typed and placed into a thick notebook. The married men had it made. Their wives did the typing for them. A recruit's weekends were usually spent studying for the upcoming Monday morning's examination.

Stars, and permits to purchase firearms, weren't issued to the new recruits until they passed the halfway mark of their training program. This, agreed the police department officials, was ample time to weed out the overzealous recruits who just wanted to get a weapon into their hands and have that special feeling of a dominating power.

On Monday morning of the fourth week, just before taking the examination, Ted Namsky, Tim Barner and Leon Bukowski sat at a long table in the lunchroom. Ted thumbed nervously through his notebook. The majority of the previous week's lectures had been on Criminal Law. This was the subject that gave him the most trouble. Ted just couldn't absorb all the material that had to be memorized.

"Hey, it's your turn to buy the coffee this morning, Ted," said Tim Barner jokingly.

Ted Namsky thought to himself that it seemed as though Tim Barner never had to study for any of the examinations. He was always cool and calm before an exam and always scored a high mark when the results were posted. It just seemed to come naturally to him. Ted could swear that Tim Barner had a photographic memory.

"Yea," interrupted Leon Bukowski, "I could use a cup of that dishwater this morning."

Ted didn't really have a taste for coffee this morning, but he obliged the wishes of his two friends. Walking over to the coffee machine, he took some change out of his pocket, dropped a few coins into the coin slot and waited. Nothing happened! He pressed the button several times. Still nothing happened! Ted's two friends watched to see what his reaction was going to be to this situation

The usual procedure, for this type of dilemma, was to give the machine a few good solid whacks. Nine out of ten times, the change would fall back down into the coin slot return cup.

"Give it a couple of good kicks," yelled Leon, laughing.

Ted stood motionless in front of the tall vending machine, feeling a little foolish and embarrassed. In the past weeks, he had witnessed several people lose their coins in these vending machines. He recalled how ridiculous they had looked standing in front of the machines, pounding on them for the return of their coins. Still, this was sort of a special morning and it disturbed him deeply that he could be taken by a simple piece of machinery. At first, Ted hit the machine with a few soft blows, just below the coin return slot. He waited, but still, nothing happened. Ted's two friends cheered him on with words of encouragement. "Kick it! Whack it! Don't let it get the best of you, Ted!"

Ted let the vending machine have a couple more blows, directly into the coin entrance slot. Still nothing happened.

By this time, other patrons in the lunchroom had joined Ted's two friends and were cheering him on with further phrases of encouragement. Ted rocked the vending machine back and forth, hoping that his money would finally drop into the slot return cup. Nothing happened. It was war! The human brain battling against a mass of wires and metal.

Without warning, the leg on the vending machine snapped. The machine fell towards the floor, narrowly missing Ted's foot. He stood motionless, red-faced and totally embarrassed. The recruits in the lunchroom laughed, cheered, clapped their hands and stomped their feet, in gestures of approval for what had just happened to the vending machine.

Ted's two friends stood up and helped him lift the coffee machine off the floor. They rested the vending machine against another vending machine. Ted got a paper napkin, scribbled the words *OUT OF ORDER* on it and placed the napkin on the front of the vending machine. He said nothing as he walked over to his table, picked up his notebook and started to leave the lunchroom, still red-faced. As he passed through the doorway, he could still hear everyone behind him cheering and clapping.

Ted passed his examination that day with a grade of 76.

CHAPTER IV

The fourth week of training, thus far, was his most interesting of all. Ted received his first introduction to the pistol range and the defensive tactics classes. He had never really fired a gun before, except for the .22 caliber rifles that he shot at carnivals.

When the range officer shouted an order to stand in the individual cubicles and prepare to load their weapons, Ted's stomach felt as though it had a nest of bees inside, beginning to stir around. They had been instructed in previous classes on how to load and fire a weapon properly, but this was the first time he was going to use real live ammunition.

Ted loaded his revolver with five live rounds of ammunition. Holding his arm out straight, he sighted his target through the small peep sight at the end of the barrel. A two-foot square target hung motionless some seventy-five yards away. It seemed an almost impossible task to hit that target.

At the range officer's command, Ted Namsky, along with the other recruits on the firing line, began firing at their targets. Ted's first four shots missed his target completely. The fifth shot managed to hit the metal clip that was holding up the target. Splinters of metal flew in every direction as the paper target fell lazily to the floor.

Ted stepped out of his cubical and looked over at the recruit in the cubical next to him. The recruit fired his revolver slowly, managing to keep both of his eyes shut. Lead bullets flew in every direction, hitting everything, except the paper target. A piece of celotex ceiling tile fell to the floor. An overhead light fixture shattered as cement chips flew up into the air from the concrete floor.

"Hold it! You dumb, knuckle headed assholes!"shouted the range officer in total frustration, "Hold it!"

The range area echoed with laughter when the lights short circuited and went out.

The following day,Ted had his first introduction to the Defensive Tactics class. It was his first class of the new day.

At precisely 7 a.m., thirty-six men changed into their gym clothes as they shivered in an ice cold locker room. The first part of the class consisted of invigorating calisthenics. The agonizing grunts, moans and groans that came from the gym were unbearable to the human ear. If someone had stood outside the gymnasium door and listened, he would have sworn that he was standing next to a medieval torture chamber. But, the real enjoyment and excitement of the Defensive Tactics classes were yet to come.

Recruits were paired off according to their height and weight. The weeks of training that followed were very educational. The instructors always used one of the recruits as his *DUMMY* to demonstrate a new defensive hold. It was the general contention of the instructor that if your arm or leg were broken, or if you dislocated your shoulder, in time, it would heal. So, they gladly demonstrated their defensive tactic holds on their waiting victims.

Tim Barner was chosen to be the *DUMMY* for the upcoming demonstration. He stood at attention as the instructor grabbed him around the neck and did a reverse turn. Tim flew through the air with the gratefulness of a swan in flight and landed with the clumsiness of an elephant, crashing through the rotting wall boards. Splinters and chunks of wood flew in every direction, leaving Tim protruding out of a four-foot hole in the wall. The sound of laughter echoed throughout the room for several minutes as Tim limped back to his position in line and sat down on the wooden floor.

"O.K., softies, get up off of the floor and pair off in partners," barked the instructor, holding his hands on his hips.

Leon Bukowski's height and weight came the closest to Ted Namsky's six-foot, two hundred and ten pound frame. They were to be partners for the remainder of their school term.

At the instructor's command, Leon grabbed his partner's wrist, twisted it and brought it around and up into the middle of his partner's back.

"Now that you've got the little darlings in a dainty pose," shouted the instructor, "toss the son-of-a-bitch down on the floor and put on the pressure hold. I want to hear the sounds of agony and pain! I want to hear it fill the room."

Leon leaned over and whispered into his partner's ear, "Do you want me to take it easy when I flip you?" he asked.

"Bullshit!" snapped Ted. "If he catches us clowning around, he'll sweat our asses off. Do what you have to do, but just don't get carried away and break my God-damn arm!"

At the instructor's command, everyone standing in the commanding position tossed their partners onto the mats, dropping their knees into the middle of their partner's backs, lifting the victim's arm up until the wrist almost touched the back of his neck. The sounds of pain echoed throughout the room, along with a few choice words that were added into the conversation - unconsciously.

The next defensive tactic hold to be taught was the combination lock and wrist toss. Ted was chosen to be the next victim. His partner positioned him for the wrist toss and followed through with the instructor's orders. As Ted flew gracefully through the air, the padded floor mats separated, leaving a six-inch gap between them. Ted's knee entered the gap and remained there, while the rest of his body continued to move forward. The muscle in his thigh tightened until it felt as though it had torn in half. Unbearable pain shot through the left side of his body.

Leon helped his partner, unable to stand up on his own, off the mats, and sat him down in the instructor's chair at the other end of the gym. The instructor, seeing Ted sitting in his chair, walked rapidly towards him.

"What in the hell's going on here?" shouted the instructor. "Are you two premadonnas tired already? Come on, get your ass out of my chair and get back on the mats!" he ordered.

"I think he injured his leg, sir," replied Leon.

"Let me have a look at it," said the instructor as he grabbed Ted's ankle and yanked. Ted let out a bellow that sounded like a blood hound baying at a full moon.

"Yeah! I guess you did injure the leg kid," said the instructor, laughing. "Have you got your car in the parking lot, Namsky?" he asked.

"Yes, I do," Ted answered.

"You know," the instructor continued, "the policy around here is that when someone gets hurt, it's his partner's responsibility to see that the injured man gets to the hospital for some kind of treatment."

"We're familiar with that regulation," remarked Leon. "I'll take Ted to the hospital."

"Then do it," ordered the instructor. "Get dressed and we'll make out an injured on duty report before you leave for the hospital."

The hospital was a short distance from the Police Academy. Leon parked the car in a reserved spot and helped his partner walk into the emergency room. A young blond haired girl sat behind the information desk. She was clad in white garments and wore the pin of a Registered Nurse.

"May I help you?" she inquired, as Ted hobbled up to the information desk.

"I think I tore something in my left thigh this morning in our judo class," he replied.

"Oh, you're one of those new hotshot police recruits from the Academy," she said laughing, then rose from her chair. "Follow me into one of our examination rooms," she ordered as she walked away from them.

Ted hunched his way slowly towards the small room into which the young nurse had gone. Upon his entrance into the room, the nurse proceeded to give him instructions.

"O.K., hotshot, drop your pants! Let me have a look at your injured area. Afterwards, you can crawl up onto that cart and cover yourself with that sheet."

An expression of embarrassment appeared on Ted's face. "I'm not going to take my pants off while you're in here, nurse," he shyly remarked.

"Well now, what have we here? A shy and embarrassed policeman!" she said, laughing. "O.K. sweetheart, have it your own way. I'll leave, but make sure you drop those pants and get up on that cart. The doctor will be in shortly to examine you. He'll probably want to take some x-rays of your leg and hip."

The young nurse left the room, closing the large plastic curtain behind her. Ted removed his gun belt and handed it to his partner. Each movement of his leg led to more unbearable pain. He unbuckled his pants belt and let his pants drop to his ankles. Suddenly, he heard a tapping noise coming from behind him. He turned around to investigate the sound. To his surprise, he discovered that the entire upper half of the wall was a continuous line of glass windows.

The young nurse had drawn the curtain to the open position. She stood there, along with seven other nurses, watching Ted Namsky undress. His face turned a bright red as he tried desperately to get his pants off the rest of the way. The pain grew more intense with each new movement of his leg. The nurses began to clap and whistle as he finally took his pants off and made his way onto the cold cart.

While the nurses cheered, they also shouted," GO-GO, Honey! Take it off! Take everything off!"

Ted lay on the cart, pulling the white sheet up to his waist, concealing his exposed legs. He rested his head on the soft white pillow. His red glowing face was illuminated against the white background of the pillow.

Officer Namsky glanced over towards the nurses, smiled and gave them a short wave of his hand. The nurses all laughed as they returned the wave and went back to their normal duties.

The middle age doctor entered the examining room and gave Ted a complete examination. He had sustained some tissue damage. That was the extent of his injuries.

CHAPTER V

The weeks of training that passed had helped Ted Namsky to become very knowledgeable about various police subjects. Another new phase of training was introduced to him. The instructors had become even more informal towards the new recruits. Greetings, such as asshole, dumbbell, stupid, idiot, polock, mick and dago, to mention a few, were constantly shouted at the students by their instructors.

The recruits were dumbfounded at first, but it didn't take them long to figure out the reason for the crude greetings. The instructors were testing the tempers of the recruits. They wanted to see just how much abuse the recruits could withstand before they blew their tops.

The Defensive Tactics class on removing a violator from his automobile was most interesting. The object of the lesson was to remove a violator from his car, when he refused to come out, without doing bodily harm or injury to yourself, or course.

By now, the eagerness, enthusiasm and determination of the recruits had risen to its highest point. A recruit was picked at random to play the part of the protesting violator. He sat himself down behind the wooden steering wheel of the make-believe car. Each recruit had to go through the motions of stopping the violator and asking him to get out of the car. After the offender refused, he was removed from the automobile, physically.

The first recruit grabbed his make-believe offender around the neck and twisted his head as though he were going to twist the neck off a chicken. The second recruit grabbed his offender around the neck and choked him until his face turned blue.

"Not that way, you dumb-ass, knuckle-head," screamed the instructor. He then demonstrated the proper holds to use on the offender. "This is the way you do it!"

The third recruit was the funniest of all. He grabbed the offender around the neck and twisted. He succeeded in lifting the make-believe offender off the car seat, but as he did, the offender's foot got stuck in the wooden steering wheel. The recruit yanked, twisted and tugged while his make-believe offender choked and his face turned different colors of the rainbow.

"Idiots!" screamed the instructor at the top of his voice. The entire class let out a roar of laughter.

Every class has its joker and this recruit class was no exception. Tony Seccoro was this class's joker.

The day of the first formal uniform and weapons inspection had arrived. The men stood milling around the locker room, getting ship-shape for their inspection. Two of the recruits had to go to the bathroom before inspection. They left their gun belts hanging in their open lockers.

Tony Seccoro was at his best that day. He removed the cartridges from the first recruit's revolver and loosened the cylinder shaft on the second recruit's gun.

Roll call was held at 9 a.m. that morning. The recruits assembled on the football field of a nearby stadium. The spit-and-shine, strict discipline lieutenant, in charge of all of the recruits at the Academy, held the inspection. The recruits paraded around the football field, to the cadence of close order drill, for two hours that day. Finally, the inspection was to be held.

At the conclusion of uniform inspection, the men were instructed to prepare for a weapons inspection. The two recruits, carrying the tampered revolvers, stood in the front row and were inspected first. The lieutenant took the revolver from the first recruit and opened the cylinder. He looked at the revolver in total disbelief. He turned it upside down to show that there were no cartridges in the cylinder.

"O.K. Just what in the hell did you do with them?"the lieutenant screamed at the recruit.

"The bullets were in there, the last time I checked my gun, sir!" replied the recruit, both nervous and embarrassed.

"I know," snapped the lieutenant. "Don't tell me! Let me guess? Your wife won't let you carry bullets in your revolver because they're dangerous and she took them out of your revolver before you left home."

"I'm not married, sir," replied the recruit.

The lieutenant returned the revolver to the recruit, remaking angrily, "Get some cartridges and load that weapon now, mister!"

The lieutenant stopped in front of the second recruit. Taking the revolver from the recruit's hand, he pressed the release bar and pushed on the cylinder. The cylinder fell out of the gun frame and landed on the ground, spilling the cartridges at the lieutenant's feet.

"Jesus Christ! I've got nothing but a bunch of dumb fuck-ups!" screamed the lieutenant. The sound of laughter could be heard throughout the entire stadium.

The recruits marched an extra two hours that day.

CHAPTER VI

The recruits were constantly harassed by the instructors. They cursed them. They yelled at them every chance they got. At the conclusion of their training, the recruits realized what all of the harassment was about. Putting a man out on the street with s short temper and a revolver in his hand was nothing but asking for trouble. Every precaution had to be taken to prevent the wrong person from being out in that street, wearing a police officer's uniform.

The final week of Police School was just a simple review of the teachings from the previous weeks. The only exception was the class on handcuffing procedures. All the recruits were in an exceptionally good mood that day. With graduation just four days away, they were feeling a little chipper and carefree.

The tall instructor stood at the head of the class, resting on the edge of the desk. He manipulated several pair of handcuffs in his hands.

"Today we're going to work on the principles of handcuffing one, two and three suspects at one time," he said. "First of all, I want you recruits to pair off by odd sizes - one short and one tall person. I want you to get the feeling of handcuffing different sized wrists. When we're finished, I want you to pair off again - even heights and even weights. I don't want these exercises made too easy. The officer portraying the offender is to put up a struggle. I don't want you people to come to blows, but give enough resistance so that the person handcuffing you has a difficult time doing it."

The instructor gave his instructions on the type of tactics to be used. The first team was chosen. The rest of the class watched as the two recruits went through their clumsy charades.

The smaller of the two grabbed the other's wrist and tried to snap on a set of handcuffs. The taller officer twisted his wrist and broke away. The smaller officer grabbed the officer's wrist again, and again the officer broke away, but this time he took three steps backwards and fell over the instructor's chair, upsetting it and the neat stack of papers that were sitting on top of the desk. The classroom instantly filled with the sound of laughter. Bending his head, the instructor shook it from side to side in disgust. "Next two people!" he grumbled.

The second team followed their instructions to the letter. After a short struggle, the smaller officer succeeded in handcuffing his partner's hands behind his back. Achieving his goal, the officer turned and faced the class, revealing a catlike smile along with a bow of his head. The handcuffed officer slowly manipulated his hands from behind his back and grabbed his partner around his neck.

The recruit gasped and choked, revealing an expression of amazement on his face. The class and instructor sat and watched in disbelief and astonishment at what they had just witnessed.

"How in the hell did you do *that*?" asked the instructor, getting up from his chair.

"I'm double-jointed in the shoulders, sir," replied the handcuffed officer. The instructor turned to face the class. "Now, take special notice of just what happened. The unexpected! Remember it! Remember it for as long as you're a cop! That could have been you up there with your prisoner. If it was, the city would probably be minus one prisoner and one cop. Anytime you take a person into custody, cuff his right hand first, bring it around to the base of his spine and if he's wearing a belt, take advantage of it. Slip the other cuff between his belt and pants, then cuff his left hand. He'd have to drop his pants to get out of that position. Of course, if he's some kind of contortionist, then, you're just shit out of luck! Remember, don't walk or stand with your back to your prisoner at any time. Make sure that you're always behind him and keep an eye on him at all times. O.K., let's pair off and try that exercise again."

Officers Namsky and Bukowski were partners again. "Make it look good, Leon," whispered Ted. "I only want to go through this once. If he sees that we're not trying, he'll keep us up here for the rest of the period, practicing."

Officer Bukowski grabbed his partner's wrist, but Ted freed himself from the grasp. Leon tried the wrist-hold again, spinning his partner around. Ted's nose collided with the blackboard. Tiny trickles of blood slowly flowed from each of Ted's nostrils.

The nurses at the hospital were happy to see Ted and his partner again, even if it was only for a short visit.

After fourteen weeks of vigorous, enlightening and educational training, the class of sixty-two recruits finally graduated. At last, they were *COPS!*

CHAPTER VII

Officers Namsky, Bukowski, Barner and Seccoro were assigned to the same District Station house. The rest of the class were distributed throughout the city.

Ted looked at his watch, then walked up to the sergeant's desk at the Raven Avenue District Station. It was 10:45 p.m.

"What can I do for you, lad?" said the silver haired sergeant.

"My name's Ted Namsky, sarge. I'm fresh out of the Academy. I was told to report here for the midnight duty watch."

"Follow those stairs up to the second floor," said the desk sergeant. "We'll be holding roll call in the squad room in about fifteen minutes."

Ted thanked the sergeant and walked up the stairway. The squad room was already crowded with chattering police officers. Ted spotted a bench with an empty space, walked over and sat down. His eyes scanned the room slowly. Men were both sitting and standing while they talked. A few patrolmen read reports while others just chatted with their partners.

Ted was nervous, but he felt good. He was looking forward to tonight. At last, he was working at a job that he really wanted and enjoyed doing. He had at last achieved one of his goals in life. He felt a little uneasy and then it dawned on him that he had to go to the bathroom. He left his new gear on the bench and went to look for the restroom. Five minutes later, when he returned to the bench, he discovered that his new flashlight, ticket book and raincoat were gone. He had actually been ripped off by one of his own kind.

"*FUCK IT!*" he shouted loudly.

Several minutes later Leon Bukowski, Tim Barner and Tony Seccoro came into the squad room. Ted was relieved to see them. At least now, he knew someone who was working the midnight shift with him. That lonely feeling disappeared.

"Don't leave your new equipment laying around guys! One of these pricks will steal it from you!" Ted shouted loud enough for everyone to hear.The watch commander and one of his field sergeants followed Ted's friends into the squad room.

Following roll call, the watch commander introduced the new men joining the midnight watch. Beat cars were assigned and special orders were read from the commanding officer's log book.

Ted was assigned to a squadrol beat, while his three friends were assigned to regular beat cars. When the men were dismissed, Ted walked up to his new partner and introduced himself.

"Hi," he said. "My name's Ted Namsky." His hand extended forward for a friendly handshake.

"Robert. Robert Mack," replied the six-foot, two hundred and forty pound officer, shaking Ted's hand. He removed his hat and wiped his forehead with a clean handkerchief. Strands of hair were very scarce on the top of his head. "Jesus Christ, it's hot in here," he said. "They must have that God-damn heat turned up all the way again," he grumbled.

"Yeah, it is kind of warm in here, now that you mention it,"Ted agreed.

"Sit down , kid," said Officer Mack. "When did you get out of the Academy?" he asked.

"I graduated Thursday night,"Ted replied as he began unzipping his leather jacket.

"You know kid, they really assigned you to a good watch to start learning the ropes. It's not everyone that gets assigned to the first watch on a Saturday night," remarked Robert Mack, jokingly. "We're working the meat wagon tonight, kid. My regular partner turned up lame tonight."

"That's a crazy name for a squadrol - meat wagon," said Ted, smiling.

"That's what the civilian population in this district call it, kid. We haul so many bodies to the morgue and hospitals, that they nicknamed our squadrol - *The Meat Wagon*. Kid, you're working in one of the busiest districts in the city, that's, as the crime rate goes. You'll learn, believe me, you'll learn fast! When we hit that street tonight, you'll be one of the city's finest, all dressed up in your pretty blues. You'll be one of the districts best - you'll serve and protect and will be the *FIRST LINE DEFENSE* out there.

This little speech made Ted feel a little uneasy. He was sure that his new partner was only ribbing him - but again, maybe he wasn't? The only thing that really bothered Ted was that he hated being called - kid. After all, he was twenty-five years old. Even if his partner was forty years old, he didn't have that many years over him to call him - kid.

"O.K., kid, bring your clipboard and some blank reports. I'll drive tonight. You're the man on the paper work. I'll show you around the district so that you'll familiarize yourself with it."

"That's O.K. with me," said Ted, getting up off the wooden bench. "Only, please do me one small favor?"

"Sure, kid. What is it?" asked Robert Mack.

"Please stop calling me kid. The name's Ted. O.K.?" requested Ted.

"Sure, kid! Anything you say," said Robert Mack, laughing, as he walked towards the doorway.

Ted shook his head in disbelief, remaining silent as they both left the squad room together.

The first few hours brought only routine assignments; a few family disturbances, a couple of traffic stops, some theft reports to be filled out, and some prisoners from a street fight who had to be transported back to the District Station.

At last, the call that proved to be the most interesting of the evening came over the car radio. "Squadrol 6798! Respond please!"

Ted quickly grabbed the microphone and replied, "Squadrol 6798."

"Go to 7-2-4- West End Street," ordered the dispatcher. "A possible homicide! Detectives on the scene."

"Ten-four," responded Officer Namsky.

Robert Mack switched on the Mars light and turned on that famous wailing siren. They sped down Wilkes Avenue heading for the street called West End.

Six patrol cars blocked the street in front of 724 West End. The revolving Mars lights lit up the entire block, waking everyone in the neighborhood. Robert Mack brought the squadrol to a stand still, next to a sergeant who was standing on the curb, talking with some patrolmen.

"What-a-ya got, Sarge?" asked Officer Mack.

"D.O.A., Mack. He's up there in that fourth floor apartment," replied the brawny sergeant, pointing towards a set of apartment windows. "Looks like a family quarrel. I would guess that the wife hit her husband in the back of the head with an axe. We can't get a statement from the wife yet. Doc says she's in a state of shock. The dick's are up there with her now, trying to get through to her. Get up there and take the body out. The lab people are through with their job. Get the body pronounced at the hospital, then take him right to the morgue, and don't forget to inventory the clothes this time. Do you understand me, Mack?"

"O.K., Sarge, O.K.," answered Officer Mack, saluting. "Come on, kid. We'll get you to handle your first stiff!"

The climb up the steep stairs to that fourth floor apartment seemed endless. The hallway was extremely narrow, besides smelling like an unflushed urinal. Robert Mack was puffing heavily when they reached the apartment.

They set the stretcher down next to the dead man's body. Several plainclothes detectives and uniformed officers stood around, discussing the reason for the man's death. Ted Namsky began to open the black plastic disaster bag.

"Never mind the bag, kid," said Robert Mack. "Just lay a lot of newspapers down on the stretcher where his head will be resting. The paper will absorb most of the blood."

Ted followed his partner's advice. They lifted the lifeless body off the floor and placed it on top of the stretcher. Robert Mack laced the web belts together so the body wouldn't slip off the stretcher.

"You take the head, kid. I'll take the feet."

"O.K.," Ted replied, already lifting the heavy stretcher. They started their long journey down the four flights of steep stairs. The other officers watched as Officers Mack and Namsky struggled with the heavy stretcher.

"You go down first," suggested Officer Mack

The watching officers knew that this was Ted Namsky's first night on the street and this was also his first encounter handling a dead body. Word gets around very fast in a district when a new policeman handles his first dead body. They used the same routine for every new patrolman.

Ted started to walk down the stairway. Robert Mack lifted the stretcher higher than it should have been lifted. The body started to slide towards Ted.

"Catch him! Don't let him slide off the stretcher!" Robert Mack shouted.

Ted lifted up his end of the stretcher, trying to level it. The dead man's head hit Ted's left cheek and came to rest on his shoulder.

At the hospital, while the doctor was pronouncing the man to be deceased, Ted went into the washroom. Turning on the water, he stared at himself in the smoke filmed mirror. Blood, along with parts of hair and skin, had dried onto his cheek and jacket. Ted leaned forward and vomited into the white porcelain sink. He continued to vomit until it felt as though his stomach was going to turn inside out!

CHAPTER VIII

The midnight and late afternoon shifts had come and gone. The day watch had finally arrived. There was some work to do on the day watch, but not as much as the other two watches. The past sixty days had been busy enough for Ted. He was grateful for the rest that he was getting. He felt like a veteran of the streets! During the past sixty days, he had handled every type of crime possible. Yes, it felt good to catch your breath on the day watch. The school crossings, traffic control and report writing was a pleasurable change.

Tuesday, of the second week, had arrived. Ted Namsky looked at his wrist watch: 9:15 a.m. He and Leon Bukowski were working as partners that week.

The last of the children had just entered the school as Leon stopped the squad car next to Ted. Ted opened the car door and got in.

"Have a busy morning, Leon?" asked Ted as he fussed with his holster.

"Had a traffic stop and one stolen auto report to fill out. That's it. Do you want to drive?"

"Nah. You drive. I'm a little tired this morning. Drive over to Taylor Street. They've had a couple of strong arm robberies and purse snatchings there in the last few weeks. Let's see if we can get lucky and catch one of them."

Officer Bukowski dropped the selector bar into the drive position and sped off towards Taylor Street.

They had just passed 32nd Street when an all-alert call came over the car radio speaker. "All cars be on the look out for a gray 1962 Ford Sedan heading south bound on Taylor Street. The suspect auto contains two armed suspects. They're wanted in connection with an armed robbery of the Greenwood Currency Exchange at 3110 South Taylor Street."

"Hell, that's only a block away from here," exclaimed Leon.

"Hey! Look at that car coming towards us," shouted Ted. "Get the hell out of his way or he'll smash right into us!"

Leon swerved the squad car just as the 1962 gray Ford Sedan sped past them, narrowly missing the left side of their squad car.

"That's them!" Ted shouted. switching on the siren and Mars light. "Turn this bucket of bolts around and let's get after them!"

Leon made a quick *U* turn and sped after the 1962 Ford. Ted grabbed the microphone and shouted, "Car 2206! Emergency! Emergency!"

"All cars stand by," came the dispatcher's reply. "Go ahead 2206."

"We're in pursuit of that 1962 gray Ford. We're heading south on Taylor Street, just passing 35th. Suspect's auto license plate number is Lincoln-Charley-6-3-7-8, Illinois. Do you read me, squad?"

"Loud and clear, 2206! Stay in pursuit and keep us informed on any change of direction," ordered the dispatcher.

The dispatcher ordered squad cars in the immediate area to start setting up road blocks.

"Look at the trunk lid of that car, Ted," Leon shouted. "See anything unusual about it?"

"Sure do! Since when do they have a tail pipe coming out of a trunk lid? I don't like the looks of it, Leon!"

The suspect car suddenly changed direction by making a sharp left turn.

"They're trying to shake us,"said Leon, making the same sharp left turn, still in pursuit of the suspect car.Ted grabbed the microphone again. "Car 2206! Suspect's vehicle now heading east bound on 46th Street. Looks like they're trying to make it to the expressway!"

"We've got the expressway entrances blocked, 2206,"answered the dispatcher.

"Don't get too close to them, Leon," remarked Ted. "There's something funny going on inside of that car. Stay back just far enough away to watch them. They're going to run into one of our road blocks, sooner or later."

The person sitting on the passenger side of the suspect vehicle stuck his head out the car window and pointed a gun at the squad car. Two puffs of blue smoke, followed by two loud cracks, echoed in the streets. The front windshield of the squad car shattered as the two lead bullets buried their way into the seat of the squad car.

Ted was hit in the face by flying glass. Tiny trickles of blood oozed out of the cuts and flowed down from his forehead, down to his chin.

"Are you all right?" screamed Leon, narrowly missing a car as they shot through an intersection.

"Yeah, I'm O.K. Just a few cuts,"said Ted. "Look, there's the entrance onto the expressway. There's two blue and whites blocking it. Oh! Oh! They're changing direction again. They're heading for the God-damn lakefront!"Ted used the microphone again. "Car 2206! Hey squad, the suspect auto is now heading for the lakefront. We're still in close pursuit."

"Ten-four, 2206," answered the dispatcher. "We've got the lakefront covered with road blocks too."

The suspect auto sped through traffic at a high rate of speed, with car 2206 in close pursuit.

"Look!" Ted shouted, "there's the beach area ahead. They're heading right for it."

Suddenly, the back end of the suspect car lit up with a great flash of light.

"Jesus Christ!"screamed Leon as the front end of their squad car lifted up into the air. Ted tried to grab onto something as the squad car bounced off a curb. The car spun around until it came to a sudden halt, as it smashed into a tree. Two other squad cars had joined in the chase by this time. The officers in the pursuing squad cars fired at the suspect auto, successfully hitting it. The suspect auto spun out of control, shot across the sandy beach and came to rest in the lake. The two suspects were taken into custody.

The back end of Beat Car 2206 belched out a puff of black smoke followed by a family of gulping bright red and yellow flames. The squad car began to burn furiously.

Two other squad cars came to a screeching stop, next to Beat Car 2206. The officers ran over to the burning squad car to see what they could do to help. The first officer to reach the burning car was Tony Seccoro. Leon and Ted sat slumped over in the front seat of the burning car;both in a semiconscious condition.

"Hey! You two idiots, get the hell out of that flaming casket before it blows to kingdom come!" screamed Tony Seccoro, trying desperately to force open one of the doors.

"Can't move," whispered Leon, in a very weak voice.

Fumbling with his door handle, Ted shook his dazed and aching head from side to side. "It's no use! I can't get it open! The door's jammed, Tony!" he shouted, hysterically. Tony Seccoro turned to his partner and shouted, "Get me that tire iron out of our trunk. And God-damn it, make it snappy! I don't think there's much time left before this car blows."

Tony Seccoro's partner did as he was told. Officer Seccoro jammed the tire iron between the door and door frame of the burning car, but none of the doors would give way to the pressure of the tire iron. Tony succeeded in bending a small portion of the top of the driver's door. "This ain't doing any damn good!" he shouted. "Charlie, back our squad car up to this door."

"It'll be too close to the fire," protested Tony Seccoro's partner.

"The hell with the fire! Just do what I tell you to do!" ordered Tony.

His partner quickly backed up their squad car to within four -feet of the burning squad car. Tony reached into the trunk of his squad car and took out the harness for catching dogs. He quickly disassembled it. Using a heavy rope, he fastened one end of the rope to the bumper of his squad car and the other end to the small opening he had made in the driver's door of the burning car.

"It won't hold! The rope will break!" yelled Officer Seccoro's partner. "If it doesn't break, we could flip their car over if we pulled too hard."

"It's the only chance we've got, isn't it? Are we gonna stand here and watch them fry in that car?" Officer Seccoro and his partner got into their squad car. Tony turned on the ignition and started the car. Dropping the selector bar into the drive position, he slowly pressed down on the accelerator pedal with his foot. His squad car slowly moved forward, taking up the slack in the rope. Tony's partner got out of their squad car.

"Is all of the slack out of the rope yet?"Tony yelled loudly to his partner.

"All out!" the reply came back.

Tony slammed the accelerator pedal to the floor.The engine roared loudly. The tires dug furiously into the dirt, throwing grass and dirt in all directions. The burning auto slid six feet on the grass. Suddenly, the driver's door, of the burning car, swung open.

"Hold it!" yelled Officer Seccoro's partner as he made a mad dash for the burning car. Tony was right behind him. They pulled Leon out first and carried him to a safe area. Two other officers pulled Ted out of the car and laid him down on the grass next to his partner.

A squadrol pulled up, next to the officers. Two stretchers were removed from the back of the squadrol and the injured officers were placed on them. Tony Seccoro stood in front of the two stretchers, his hands resting on his slender hips. He looked down at the two injured officers. Ted Namsky slowly opened his eye lids and looked up at Tony. "Thanks, buddy," he whispered softly.

Tony laughed quietly and replied, "Boy! When you two guys do something, you really do it up big. I thought I was the only one who could get himself into a really good jam. Do you know what those guys had sticking out of that trunk lid? A 20MM Recoilless Rifle! That's what hit the street in front of your squad car. You guys were sure lucky!"

At that moment, Beat Car 2206 exploded and burst into a volley of flames. Ted closed his eyes again. He formed a little smile on his lips as the officers lifted up his stretcher and placed it into the back of the squadrol. The officers turned on the Mars lights and siren, then drove off in the direction of Christian Hospital.

CHAPTER IX

Three months of healing for Ted Namsky's injuries, was ample time enough. Leon Bukowski's fractured ankle and knee cap took a little longer to heal.

Ted was back on the midnight watch. Roll call had just been concluded. Special car assignments and instructions were handed out to the men. Ted and Tony were assigned as partners for the entire work period. If Ted had only known what he was heading for during this watch period, he'd have stayed on the medical roll.

"Who drives tonight?" asked Ted as he and Tony walked out to their assigned squad car.

"I'll drive," replied Tony. "I don't feel much like writing tonight. You handle the paper work and I'll handle the steering wheel." Ted shrugged his shoulders in an approving manner and threw his partner the car keys.

The night air was warm. It felt good to be back in uniform and working again, thought Ted. He tried to keep the last experience in a squad car out of his mind, but the fear of it recurring was still there! Ted knew that it would take a very long time for the uneasiness to go away.

Routine calls filled the first three hours of duty: family disputes, traffic violations, arresting drunks and picking up the street walkers.

"Hey!" said Tony. "How about going down to the railroad yards and shooting some rats? I've got my pellet gun in my attaché case."

"O.K. with me," answered Ted. "It'll help to make the night pass faster."

Officer Seccoro drove west bound down Logan Street until they came to the entrance to the railroad freight yards. The rear end of the squad car bounced vigorously as they rolled over the metal rails. Tony parked the squad car next to a patch of waist-high weeds. Directly across the road from them was a ten-foot stack of old wooden railroad ties.

"We'll wait here awhile. I've been to this spot before," said Tony. "The rats usually crawl along those wooden ties. When we hear them, turn on the spotlight. I'll shoot at them with the pellet gun. The spotlight blinds them and they freeze in their tracks. They're a lot easier to hit that way."

The two officers waited fifteen minutes before they heard the first scratching sounds from the wood pile. "There he is, over there!" whispered Tony, taking aim with the pellet gun.

"Where?" asked Ted, trying to focus his eyes on the wood pile.

"Look at the top board - on the left! When I tell you, switch on the spotlight. Get ready! Now!" shouted Tony.

Ted switched on the spotlight, directing the beam of light straight for the rat. The rat froze in its tracks. Tony slowly squeezed the trigger. A loud popping sound echoed in the quiet night. The rat flew two feet into the air, spun around and disappeared behind the wood pile.

"Got him!" Tony shouted. Ted turned off the spotlight. Ten minutes later, they heard some more scratching noises coming from the wood pile. Ted turned on the spotlight again.

"Aw, hell!" said Tony, disgustedly. "It's only a God-damn cat!" At that same moment, the dispatcher paged their call number over the car radio: "Car 2217!"

"2217," Ted answered.

"A burglary in progress at 2418 Logan Street. Two possible suspects in the building right now."

"Got it, squad! We're on our way!" said Ted.

Tony tucked the pellet gun inside his waist band, next to his belly button. He started the squad car and made a sharp *U* turn. The squad car bounced violently as it went over the metal rails. Both officers bounced up and down in the front seat of the car. Passing over the last piece of track, as they were coming back down on the car seat, the pellet gun fired! There was a soft *POP* and a quiet *HISSSSSSS* of escaping gas, just before Tony's scream of agonizing pain!

"It didn't?" exclaimed Ted, starting to laugh.

"Son-of-a-bitch! It did!" shouted Tony, removing the pellet gun from his waist band, grabbing himself by the crotch of his pants, in horrible pain."

"Where did you get hit?"asked Ted, trying to keep from choking as he laughed loudly.

"I don't know," Tony answered. "I'm all numb. Get me to a God-damn hospital! Right away!"

Tony slid over to the passenger side of the squad car, while Ted moved behind the steering wheel. He picked up the microphone: "Car 2217!"

"Go ahead, 2217," answered the dispatcher.

"Squad," Ted paused, "reassign our call to another car. My partner was just taken ill. I'm taking him to the emergency room at Christian Hospital."

"Is he sick enough to require a squadrol for transportation," asked the dispatcher

"No, I can handle it, squad," replied Ted.

"Ten-four, 2217. I'll send a supervisor to meet you at the hospital," said the dispatcher. Ten minutes later they were at the hospital.

"What's wrong with Seccoro?"asked the sergeant as he sat down in a chair. Ted explained the whole story as it happened. At the conclusion of the sergeant's investigation of the *accident*, Officer Seccoro and a doctor came out of a small room.

"How is he, Doc?"asked the sergeant, standing up.

"He'll feel some pain for a day or two,"said the doctor."The pellet grazed his penis and lodged itself inside of the testicle sack. No vital organs were injured. I had to lance the sack and do a little probing for the pellet, but I got it out. It took six stitches to close up the hole. We gave him a tetanus shot. He'll be all right in a couple of days." The doctor turned towards Tony. "I suggest you stay away from any women for at least a week or two!" The three officers laughed as the doctor walked away.

"How much time-due have you got on the books, Seccoro?" asked the sergeant.

"A couple of days, Sarge,"Tony answered, taking a painful step forward.

"You're off the next two days, aren't you?" the sergeant asked again.

"Yeah, Sarge. Why?"

"We've only a couple of hours left on the watch. Why don't you take the rest of the watch off. I'll carry you as sick for the rest of the watch. You can rest up for the next couple of days. If you still don't feel well when you're due back on duty, give me a call and we'll arrange a couple of time-due days for you."

"Thanks, Sarge, I'll do just that," replied Tony, walking painfully out to the squad car.

"Namsky," continued the sergeant, "give Seccoro a lift back to his car, then come back up on the air as a one-man car."

"Right, Sarge,"said Ted as he started walking towards his squad car.

"*HEY! SECCORO!*"yelled the sergeant.

"Yeah, Sarge," Tony answered, as he turned around to face the sergeant.

"Do me a favor, will you?"said the sergeant, laughing, "and get rid of that God-damn pellet gun!"

"Get rid of the pellet gun?" said Tony. "Sure, Sarge, sure!"he answered. Tony turned around and straddle-walked very slowly back to the squad car.

CHAPTER X

Tim Barner was the relief man on car 2217. While Tony Seccoro was recuperating, Tim Barner and Ted Namsky worked the car together. It felt good to work with an old Academy classmate. The two of them could hash over the funny incidents that had happened at the Academy.

Roll call was over. The two officers entered Beat Car 2217. Ted wanted to drive tonight. His partner gave him no opposition. Ted started the squad car and drove towards Tornsen Avenue. The assignment calls were very slow in coming -- that was the usual trend on Monday through Thursday. You'd get a little chance to catch your breath. But, on Friday, Saturday and Sunday nights, you'd work your ass off. This was just another typical Tuesday night.

The steady hum of the wheels on the asphalt pavement made one drowsy in the early morning hours. These two officers were no exception.
After three hours of steady patrol, Ted parked the squad car next to a curb.

"Let's park here for awhile, Tim, and play that stop sign. I haven't given a ticket all week and the sergeant's been on my ass about it," said Ted, yawning.

"Are you sure you won't fall asleep?" asked Tim.

"I'm all right." Ted yawned again. "Go ahead and catch a few winks. I'll watch the stop sign and listen to the radio for the calls."

Tim slid down into the seat and closed his eyes. A short time later, Ted rolled up his window and rested his eyes - just for a few short minutes. When the beat sergeant stopped his car next to theirs, a half hour later, Ted was hunched over, his forehead resting peacefully on the steering wheel. The doors of their squad car were locked and the engine was running.

The beat sergeant pounded angrily on the driver's window with his fist, trying to arouse the two sleeping officers.

"Hey! You two guys all right in there?" he yelled. The loud shouting and pounding on the car window woke Ted, but he didn't stir. He opened his eyes slowly, trying to get his bearings. He couldn't remember where he was! Ted looked up from the corner of his eye and saw the chevrons on the sergeant's sleeve. Ted slowly lifted his head and rolled down the side window. Tim jumped up when the sergeant yelled, "What the hell are you two guys doing? Sleeping?"

Ted looked directly at the sergeant and quietly replied, "Not sleeping, Sarge! I was just praying - just praying!"

The sergeant silently laughed to himself as he spoke. "All right, get this tin can rolling - and do your praying in church from now on, Namsky!"

"Sure, Sarge, sure," replied Ted, giving the sergeant a quick salute. He put the selector bar into drive and drove off, south bound down Thornsen Street.

"2217!" came the dispatcher's call some thirty minutes later.

"2217," said Ted into the microphone.

"Go to Troller and James Streets. Give your adjoining district an assist. They have some burglary suspects trapped in a tavern."

"Ten-four!" said Ted, ending the message.

They drove for several blocks, then made a quick right turn. Ahead of them, they could see the spinning Mars lights from the many squad cars that were parked. The rapid thunder of gunfire echoed into the night air. Ted stopped the squad car a hundred feet from the tavern that was giving cover to the trapped burglars.

Officers Namsky and Barner exited their car, drew their revolvers and pointed them towards the tavern as they squatted down for protection behind the front fender of their squad car. One minute later another squad car screeched to a stop in front of their line of fire. A tall, stocky middle aged police officer got out of the car. He wore no hat or helmet for protection. His salt-and-pepper colored hair swung back and forth over his eyes. The officer quickly unfastened his holster strap and drew out the .357 magnum revolver that rested inside the holster.

As the officer brought up the revolver, it went off! The metal projectile violently tore its way through the car roof and exited out the back window. "Jesus Christ Almighty! May the good saints preserve us!" screamed the surprised stocky officer. He quickly got back into his squad car, started the engine, made a quick "U" turn and backed the squad car up to its original position so that the hole in the roof looked as though it were made by one of the suspects firing from the tavern. The stocky officer got out of his squad car just before the patrol sergeant pulled up.

"Hey, Sarge!" the officer yelled, waving his hand frantically, trying to catch the sergeant's attention. Finally, he was successful.

"Look what they did to my squad, Sarge," he shouted loudly for everyone to hear.

"Get your big carcass down behind that squad car, Sweeny, before they blow your ass off!" the sergeant yelled back.

A police lieutenant came running from around the corner building and motioned for Ted and his partner to follow him. Ted and Tim got into their squad car, backed it up, then turned the corner. The lieutenant stopped them as they approached the alley.

"Cover this alley entrance and make sure they don't come out the back way of the tavern!" he ordered.

"Right, Lieutenant!" said Ted, driving the car into the alley entrance. Ted and Tim got out of the squad car and ran towards the back door of the tavern. As they ran, the door suddenly flew open. A tall, thin man stepped out into the alley. He held a revolver in each hand.

Tim fell to the ground, resting on his stomach. He quickly rolled over and hid behind a garbage can for protection. Ted fell to the ground and crawled behind a wooden telephone pole, tearing a hole in each knee of his slacks when he hit the concrete pavement. The male suspect fired both weapons at Ted. Ted could hear the small metal bullets burrowing their way into the wooden pole, trying desperately to get at him. The suspect turned and ran back through the doorway that led into the tavern.

Both officers returned the gunfire, chopping chips of wood out of the back of the building. For a short time, there was only silence, then a barrage of gunfire echoed from within the building. An officer came over to them and told Tim and Ted that all three suspects were dead. When they had tried to make their escape through the back door, many officers rushed through the front entrance of the tavern. When the suspects came back into the building, they ran snap-dab into the waiting officers. There was a short gun battle. One officer was wounded, but the three suspects were killed.

Ted and his partner filled out their paper work, explaining their part in the apprehension of the suspects. Two hours later they were back on patrol in their own district.

CHAPTER XI

Saturday night! One of the busiest nights of the weekend. Officers Namsky and Barner filled their squad car with gas and checked the oil level. Minutes later they were out on the streets - patrolling them.

"Car 2217!" blared the dispatcher's voice over the radio speaker.

"2217," Ted responded.

"Investigate a theft from auto at Christian Hospital. See the officer assigned there!" ordered the dispatcher.

"Ten-four, squad," answered Ted. He dropped the microphone into a small metal holder attached to the dashboard.

"Looks like it's gonna be one of those nights,Ted,"said Tim. He drove the squad car in the direction of Christian Hospital.

Tim parked the car in the small parking lot in back of the hospital, next to the emergency doors entrance. A short, burly built officer stood in the doorway, his hands resting on his hips.

"Hi, Bruno," said Ted, exiting the car. "What have you got for us?" he asked.

"It's about time you two assholes got here!" Officer Bruno Gardner answered angrily. "Where have you two been? Flirting around with some of the street whores?"

"We just got the call, Bruno."Tim replied."What're you so hot about?"

"What am I so hot about?" shouted Officer Gardner. "Come here and I'll show you what I'm so hot about!"

The two officers followed Officer Gardner over to a new Cadillac. All four tires were gone. The wheel drums rested on the asphalt pavement.

"See that?" shouted Bruno, pointing to the empty wheel drums.

"Boy, I feel sorry for that poor slob who comes out of the hospital and finds all of his tires missing," Tim remarked, laughing.

Bruno stared straight into Tim's eyes and said, "That poor dumb slob is me!"

You?" remarked Ted, surprised. "When did you get this car?"

"I bought it just this morning. Bruno answered. "I'm not sitting more than fifty feet away from this car and somebody swipes my three hundred dollar set of tires. Doesn't that just frost your ass?"

"Take it easy, Bruno!" said Tim. "Without the tires, look at the wear that you'll save on the car. You can always sit and admire it."

"Screw you, Barner!" shouted Bruno. "Now get your ass inside and fill out that report. I'm gonna need it for my insurance company."

The three officers walked through the hospital entrance doors, down a long corridor and into a small room that the officers used for writing reports. Halfway down the corridor, Ted stopped to admire statues and pictures of black saints hanging on the walls.

"Hey, Bruno, is this some of your handy work?" Ted asked, hysterical with laughter. The head portion of every statue had been covered with a paper sack. Every picture had bandages covering the eyes and mouth.

"Yeah, that's some of my handy work," laughed Bruno. "Every time I draw this duty assignment, I drive the Mother Superior nuts! She comes down the stairs to the hospital after morning chapel and you should see her blow her stack when see sees the statues and paintings. It breaks me up every time I see it happen."

The three officers laughed as they entered the report room. Ted started the report. A few minutes had passed when one of the new nurses came running into the room. Her bright blue eyes were as big as shiny new half dollar coins. She drew short breaths and gasped as she tried desperately to talk.

"Officer Gardner!" she finally shouted, excitedly. "There's going to be a problem in a few minutes!"

"What's the trouble, Tracy?" Bruno asked, concerned by the nurse's excited condition. He stood up and offered her his chair.

"There are several young men outside the hospital who want to visit one of their friends," she explained. "We told them that visiting hours are over, but they became belligerent and started cursing at us. They finally went outside, where they are right now."

"Which patient did they want to see, Tracy?" asked Officer Gardner.

"The Tom Watson boy."

"Oh yes, *that* boy," replied Bruno.

"Is he someone special?" Ted asked, looking up as he finished writing the report."

"He's the kid who was shot in that burglary attempt tonight over on Ashland. We have a guard on him right now until he can post a bond. I'm sure glad you two are here. I'm gonna go out and have a talk with them. You two be ready to back me up if there's a problem, O.K.?"

"Sure, Bruno," agreed both officers as they stood up. "Just lead the way and we shall follow, O' Great Bawana!" said Ted, laughing.

"Screw you two," Bruno whispered to himself, not wanting nurse Tracy Tate to hear him.

The nurse and three officers had just entered the hospital lobby when a metal garbage can came crashing through the plate glass window. Shards, as well as chunks of glass, flew in every direction. Four young men dressed in T-shirts, dungarees and black leather jackets ran into the lobby through the large gaping hole in the window. Each man carried weapons of some kind - broken tree limbs, a knife and rocks.They began smashing statues, chairs and pictures.

Ted grabbed Tracy Tate's arm and pulled her against the wall.

"Call our Communications Center and have them send over a few more cars," insisted Ted, trying to coax Tracy to hurry to the telephone. Tracy complied and quickly made the telephone call.

"All right - freeze! This is the police!"Tim Barner ordered as he walked towards the four youths.

"Freeze your ass!"came back a reply from one of the boys as he picked up a chair and swung it at Tim. The chair caught Tim on the side of his head, sending him collapsing to the floor and his gun went sliding under a couch. The boy then smashed the wooden chair into the wall, shattering it into flying pieces of wood splinters. A large section of wood hit Ted in the cheek, causing a small laceration.

The young men began to make their escape in different directions. As one of them ran past Ted, Ted grabbed his arm and stuck the barrel of his gun into the boy's ear.

"Make one false move, asshole and your eyeballs will look like the turning wheels on a slot machine!" Ted forced his prisoner to face the wall. "Now, drop that knife and let it hit the floor!"

After the boy complied with Ted's orders, Ted removed the barrel of his revolver from the boy's ear. He gave him a quick search for other weapons, then handcuffed him.

In the meantime, the other youths were apprehended by the officers who had responded to their call for help. The main lobby of the hospital was in a shambles. Broken debris lay scattered everywhere.

"Take them down to the station and put them in the lockup," said Ted. "I'll be there shortly to fill out the complaint and arrest reports. I've a few things to take care of here first.'"

Ted felt his cheek, then looked at the blood on his finger tips. He removed a handkerchief from his pocket. Tracy Tate stopped him from using it. She carefully examined the laceration and said, "Did I do all right, Officer?"

"You sure did!" said Ted, smiling in approval.

"Does the cut hurt much?" she asked.

"No, not very much," he replied.

"Come with me," she said, taking hold of his arm, leading him towards one of the treatment rooms. "I'll clean up that cut for you."

Ted sat down on top of a small metal stool, while the petite nurse moved around the room, gathering supplies to clean the laceration. She poured a little alcohol on top of a cotton ball and began wiping the blood away from the cut, touching the cut , occasionally. Ted flinched from the sting of the medication and automatically grabbed hold of the nurse's wrist.

Officers Gardner, Bukowski and Barner stood in the doorway, watching Ted and the sexy nurse.

"Hey-Hey! What have we here?" asked Leon, laughing. "A hand holding session going on while crime waits to be stopped out on those dark desolate streets?"

"Just in case you two haven't been properly introduced,"Bruno interrupted, "I'd like to do the honors now. Tracy Tate meet Officer Ted Namsky."

The young nurse smiled as she dabbed the cotton ball tenderly on the cut on Ted's face. "Hi, Ted, glad to meet you," she said.

Ted returned the smile. "Hi, Tracy. Same here."

After Tracy finished dressing the wound, Ted spoke to Tim. "How's the head, Tim? Hurt much?" he asked.

"Just a little." Officer Barner touched the small bandage on the side of his head with his finger tips. "I'm gonna go over to the station and begin filling out that paper work."

"Tell you what, Tim," interrupted Ted. "Ride back to the station in Leon's squad car. I'll drive back in ours when I'm finished here and I'll help you finish those reports, O.K.?"

"O.K. with me, buddy," Tim answered as he started to leave the hospital.

The nurse placed a small bandage over the cut. Ted took hold of Tracy's hand. "Say, your hands really are soft and tender." he said. She pulled her hand free from his grasp, remarking, "Thanks." She quickly walked over to the other side of the room.

Leon Bukowski watched the rhythmic motion of her curvaceous buttocks as they swayed from side to side.

"Say, I'll bet her hands aren't the only parts of her body that are soft and tender! he said and laughed.

Tracy stopped, turned and looked back at the three officers admiring her posterior. "Everything I own is soft and tender," she replied. "Just make sure you only admire and don't try to touch!" Everyone, including the nurse, laughed.

"Hey, no kidding. We'd better get over to the station," said Tim. "We've a hell of a lot to do. See you later, Ted."

"Yeah! I'll catch you guys in a little while," he replied.

The two officers left, leaving Ted and Tracy alone in the treatment room.

"Is the small cafeteria still open, Tracy?" he asked. "I sure could use a good hot cup of coffee along with some pleasant company. How about it? Will you join me?

"Tracy smiled. "Sure. Why not? It's almost break time anyway."

They left the treatment room. Walking along the corridor together, Ted put his arm around her, placing his hand on her shoulder. She looked at him and said, "Remember what I said back there in the treatment room. Make sure your hand doesn't go down below my shoulder blades!"

They both laughed as they entered the small cafeteria.

CHAPTER XII

Tony Seccoro was back for duty. He was assigned to work with Ted Namsky and Leon Bukowski. The midnight watch tour was over. They were into the second week of the afternoon watch. Leon was on his regular day off. Officers Namsky and Seccoro were approaching their last two hours for this day's tour of duty.

"Car 2217!" paged the dispatcher.

"2217!" Ted answered.

"2217, we have a burglary in progress at 268 South Foster street. 2218 will be your back up," said the dispatcher.

"Ten-four, squad! Let's go, Tony!" he said, turning on the Mars lights on top of the car. "We'll leave the siren off this time."

The squad car sped towards Foster Street. The two hundred block of Foster Street consisted of factories and office buildings. Beat car 2218 was already parked in front of the 268 building when Ted and Tony pulled up. Officers Tony James and Ralph Wilson stood in front of an open office door.

"What have you got?" asked Officer Seccoro.

"It's a real weird one," answered Officer James. "When we turned the corner, we saw this guy standing in this doorway. He's just standing there with his hands in his front pockets. When he spots us, he takes his hands out of his pockets and waves at us. Then, he runs down that alley and disappears. We checked out the building. There's no one inside."

Other squad cars began entering the crime area.

"Did you canvass any of the outside area?" asked Ted.

"Not yet," replied Officer Wilson. "We were waiting for you guys to get here."

"O.K., we got the paper work on this one," said Ted. "We'll start checking out the alley first. We'll take the right side and you two take the left. I'll call Communications for some cars to check out the rest of the area around the factories. He's around here somewhere. He didn't have enough time to get away from us."

The officers began the tedious job of searching - garages, yards and gangways. Officers Seccoro and Namsky stopped to check a darkened area in the alley. The rest of the alley had been illuminated by moon light, except for this one section of alley way.

"Did you bring the flashlight?" asked Ted.

"Shit!" exclaimed Tony. "I left it back in the squad car. Want me to go back and get it?"

"You'd better. Looks like there's a dead end at the other end of this alley. It's darker than hell down there."

Tony ran back to the car while Ted continued to search. Getting a firm grip on his revolver, Ted plunged deeper into the darkness of the alley. As he approached a cluster of metal garbage cans, one of the lids popped into the air and fell to the ground. A tall, dark figure emerged from inside the can. There was a moment of silence as the two men stood there looking at each other.

Tony came up behind Ted Namsky and placed the flashlight's beam on the tall stranger.

"Hi!" said the stranger, smiling. "Are you guys looking for me?" he asked.

"I'll be Goddamned,"laughed Tony. "He's a nut. Nothing but a screwball. O.K. pal, let's go!" ordered Tony.

"I can't make my legs move, Tony," said Ted. "That asshole scared the shit out of me!"

"You'll be all right after a good night's sleep," laughed Tony as they led the suspect out of the alley.

The locker room buzzed with the tales of their night's encounters. Changing into their civilian clothes, Officers Seccoro, Wilson and James sat on a wooden bench and laughed at the way the psycho had scared the hell out of Ted Namsky.

"O.K., just cool it, guys!" pleaded Ted, knowing that when the word got around the whole district, he'd have a lot more ribbing to contend with.

"Hey, Ted. How goes it with you and that new nurse at Christian Hospital? Oh, I forget he name," said Officer James.

"Tracy. Tracy Tate's her name," Ted answered. "I'm doing great with her. I've got a date with her and I intend to date her as many times as I can in the next two weeks."

"Oh, we've got a real hot romance story starting here, guys," Tony Seccoro butted in and laughed loudly.

"Aw, cut it out, Tony." Ted interrupted. He stood up from the bench and slipped on his civilian pants. "I'm serious about the girl. I'm on duty tomorrow night, but I sure could use the night off. I got some tickets from a friend for a really great play. The only problem is the tickets are only good for tomorrow night. Tracy's off, and I really would like to take her to see the play. You know the scene - a good play...then out to a nice restaurant for some good food... some soft music... dancing.... And, *who knows* what can happen after that?"

"No kidding," interrupted Tony, sounding excited. "Do you really think that you and Tracy might get hitched in the future?"

"You never can tell, Tony. I really feel that Tracy's the right one for me. It's hard to explain, but sometimes you meet someone and you both just know that you were meant to be together from that very first moment," Ted answered seriously.

"Ted, tell you what,"interrupted Ralph Wilson."My day off is tomorrow, but I'd like to play Cupid, besides wanting to build up some extra time on the books for my baby furlough. I want to take the wife and kids to Disneyland for a few days. If you can square it with the Captain, I'll work your shift with Tony tomorrow night."

"Would you? That's great!" Ted declared, excited at the thought. "I'll speak with the captain right now before he leaves the station."

Ted returned ten minutes later with the Captain's approval.

CHAPTER XIII

The play ended with a thunderous ovation for the entire cast. Ted and Tracy squeezed their way through the theater crowd.

"Where do we go from here?" Tracy asked, tightly squeezing his hand in hers.

"Since we don't do this every night, and it is a special night for a special occasion, we're going to the Shanghai Club for a nice dinner and some dancing."

"What special occasion?" she asked, puzzled.

"Aw-aw-aw! You ask too many questions, young lady," he said, laughing as he touched her nose with the tip of his index finger. "In due time, I will tell you. In due time. What did you think of the play?"

"It was lovely," she answered. "I don't know when I've enjoyed a play as much as I did tonight."

The walk back to the parking lot was a short one. While the attendant went to get the car, Ted put his arm around Tracy's waist, pulled her towards him and gently kissed her on the lips.

"What's that for?" she whispered softly.

"I don't know. Maybe it's because I'm falling in love with you? Did you object to the kiss?" he asked.

Tracy smiled without replying, then returned the kiss.

The Shanghai Club was crowded when they arrived. Most of the theater crowd seemed to have had the same idea. Ted and Tracy were escorted to a table in a cozy corner of the room.

"Will this table do, Tracy?" he asked. "If not, I'll get us a table closer to the dance floor."

"No, this is fine," she replied, smiling. "I like where we are."

The waiter took their order, then brought them some cocktails.

"Now," she asked, "what's the special secret?" She took a small sip from her glass. Ted hesitated a moment, then said, "What do you think of the name, Namsky?"

"I think it's a beautiful name," she answered instantly. "You're not thinking of changing it, are you?"

"No," he smiled. "I'm not, but I would like you to think about changing *your* name to Namsky." he answered, seriously.

Tracy almost dropped her glass, astonished by his announcement.

"Did I hear you correctly, Ted, " she asked, nervously.

"You heard me right, Tracy! " he answered. "From the first moment I met you, I fell in love with you. I felt - no, I knew that we were meant for each other - for all times. You were meant to belong to me, and I, to belong to no one but you."

Ted removed a small box from his suit coat pocket. He opened the small lid and handed the box to her. The illumination in the room was just right. Short bursts of light shot out from all sides of the large diamond that rested in the center of box. Tracy took the box and admired the ring for a long time without saying a single word. Finally, she spoke. "Ted, " she said, "I don't know what to say. You've taken me completely by surprise!"

"Don't say anything, Tracy, " he whispered softly, holding her hand. "If you can't speak, then just nod your head. Only, answer 'Yes' to the question that I'm going to ask you. Will you marry me?"

Tracy couldn't speak or look at Ted. The lump in her throat wouldn't let her. She kept staring down at the ring in the small box. After a short time, she closed the lid and looked directly at Ted. Her eyes sparkled as tiny droplets of water flowed lazily down her cheeks.

"Are those tears of happiness? " he asked, taking hold of her other hand, squeezing them both tightly in his own.

"No," she replied quietly. "They're tears of rejection."

"I...I don't understand. Don't you want to be with me always, too?"

"Yes, yes I do, Ted,"she answered as she handed the box back to him.

"I don't understand this,"he said sharply. "Maybe you'd better explain. I seemed to have missed something, somewhere along the line."

"Ted, I do love you, but I could never marry you as long...." Tracy hesitated for a moment, then continued. "As long as you're a policeman! I could never cope with, or live the life of a policeman's wife!"

"Tracy, you're talking silly now, " he interrupted her.

"No, I'm not!" she snapped, then started to cry.

"Look, Tracy," he whispered softly, trying to calm her shaking hand. "There are over fifteen thousand men in the police department. I would safely say that about eighty percent of them are married. Their wives and children manage to grin and bear it with no problem. They're making a go of it. Why couldn't we make a go of it, too?"

"Because," she continued to sob, "they're not in the same position that I'm in. Day after day, I see policemen come into the hospital all cut up and bruised. At the other hospital I was working at, I even saw several policemen...die! They died on the operating table from w ounds they received while doing their so-called duty. Don't you see, every time someone would say they were bringing in an injured policeman, I'd dread the thought that it was *you*. It would be like living on pins and needles everyday!"

The waiter brought their food to the table.

"Let's eat," he said dejectedly. "We'll talk about it later." They picked at their steaks. Neither one ate or enjoyed, very much of the meal...

"The night air was warm and gentle as it quickly blew past them, touching their faces. They drove along the Outer drive, on the Lakefront. The water looked dark and dangerous, but inviting to wade in. Ted finally broke the silence.

"Let's stop and park by the beach. We can walk in the water and on the warm sand, if you like."

"All the talking we do is not going to change my mind, Ted. I told you how I felt back at the restaurant. Ted, as long as you're a police officer, a marriage between us will *not* happen. So just forget it. What time is it?" she asked.

Ted looked at his watch. "A quarter to two."

"You'd better take me home, Ted. I start on the noon shift tomorrow and I'll need a little sleep before I go in to work."

A small smile formed on Ted's lips. "Well," he said, "you can't shoot a man for trying."

"No, you can't," she whispered, then touched his face tenderly with her finger tips.

"You know that I'm going to keep on proposing to you,"he said, smiling.

"Oh, I expect you too. Who knows, maybe one day, in deep desperation, you'll get lucky and I'll say 'Yes'." They both laughed at her remark.

"Do you mind if we drive through the district on the way home?" he asked. "I'd like to see what's happening there tonight."

"No, I don't mind," she replied.

The screaming wail of an overworked siren could be heard in the distance. Ted looked into his rear view mirror and saw the approaching Mars lights behind him. The vehicle was approaching at high speed. Ted pulled his car over towards the curb and waited until the squad cars passed him. Taking a quick passing glance, Ted saw Leon Bukowski and Ralph Wilson riding in one of the squad cars.

"Do you mind if we follow them?" he asked, excitedly. "I'd like to see what's happening."

"Just as long as it doesn't take too long, Ted. I have to get some sleep," she insisted.

Ted put the selector bar into the drive position and sped off after the flashing Mars lights. The spinning blue lights led him to the parking lot of St. Robert's Church. Ted parked his car, then got out.

"Wait here,Tracy. I'll only be a moment,"he said, talking to her through the open driver's window. He turned and walked towards a group of talking police officers.

Leon Bukowski saw Ted approaching him. "Hey, old buddy!" he said. "What are you doing up so late? Take Tracy home already?"

"No, Tracy's sitting in my car. What's going on, Leon?"

"We got a burglary-in-progress call, Ted. Ralph Wilson and two other officers are checking out the inside of the church right now. We stayed out here to cover the doors, windows and roof, just in case the burglars tried to get away by one of those exits. But, it looks like they already flew the scene."

"Hey! Bukowski," yelled a sergeant from across the parking lot.

"Over here, Sarge," Leon answered, raising his hand into the air.

The sergeant ran over to the small group of officers. "Hi, Namsky," he said. "What are you doing here? You're not supposed to be answering calls on your day off."

"Just passing by, Sarge. I wanted to see what was happening."

"Got something hot for us, Sarge?" asked Leon.

"Don't really know if it is or not. The Communications Center just got an anonymous telephone call. The caller said there is a live bomb planted inside the church. Personally, I think it's just another of those crank callers. Probably someone sitting in their darkened living room right now, getting his or her jollies off. Anyway, the bomb squad has been notified and they're on their way right now."

The sergeant looked around the area. "Where's your partner, Bukowski?" he asked.

"Ralph and two other officers went inside the church to have a look around," Leon replied.

"Go and tell them to get their Goddamn asses out of there 'till that area has been cleared!" ordered the sergeant.

"I'll go." Ted volunteered. He ran towards the entrance doors of the church.

As he approached within twenty feet of the church doors, there was a bright flash, followed by a loud explosion. Windows shattered and the glass slivers flew in every direction. Burning debris shot up into the air. Ted was thrown to the ground by the shock wave that followed the explosion. Screams of pain came from inside the church. Then smoke, small fires and silence... Ted lay on the asphalt pavement, trying to gather his faculties. Finally coming to his senses, he realized what had happened. The bomb had exploded inside the church!

Ted lifted himself off the pavement. He was the first officer to enter the damaged church. A heavy stagnant mist hung in the air, motionless. The sound of burning, crackling wood came from everywhere. Small fires flickered in different corners of the church. A huge wooden cross that once hung over a golden tabernacle, now lay over a smashed metal alter railing. Officers began searching through the debris.

"How many guys are supposed to be in here?" shouted one of the searching officers.

"Three!" yelled Ted. "Three of them came inside the church!"

Ted began climbing over the overturned pews. He stumbled on a partly smashed head from one of the Holy Statues that had fallen off its pedestal, smashing to pieces when it hit the floor."

"Here's one of them over here!" shouted one of the searchers.

"Here's another one!" shouted another searcher.

Ted pushed his way through the debris until he reached the injured officers. Neither one was Ralph Wilson.

"They're in shock, but they're still alive,"said one of the officers. "How many did you say were in here?" he asked again.

"Three," Ted answered, turning around to continue his search for Ralph Wilson.

Ted saw the brim of a police hat sticking out from under one of the overturned pews. He moved the pew and picked up the hat. He felt the hat. It was saturated with blood! He read the number on the emblem shield. It was Ralph Wilson's hat!

"Ralph -- Ralph Wilson!" Ted shouted. "*WHERE IN THE HELL ARE YOU? HEY BUDDY, GIVE US SOME KIND OF A SIGN SO WE CAN FIND YOU. MAKE A SOUND! MOVE A BOARD! ANYTHING! JUST LET US KNOW WHERE YOU'RE AT!*"

"I found him - or what's left of him,"said one of the searching officers, sickened by the sight that lay before him. The officer stood next to what once had been a confessional booth.

Tracy Tate sat impatiently waiting in the car, nervously watching the activities of the officers in the parking lot. Ted finally came out of the church. He walked over to the sergeant. Ted gave the sergeant the object that was clutched tightly against his chest, then walked unsteadily towards his car. The sergeant stared at the blood soaked hat that he held in his hands.

Sitting down in the driver seat, Ted grasped the steering wheel tightly with both his hands. His suit was covered with dust and blood stains. The stench of smoke that clung to his clothing burned Tracy's nostrils every time she took a breath. Ted stared into space without uttering a single word.

"Is that blood on your hands and clothes?" Tracy asked, rubbing his hand with hers. "Are you all right, Ted? Are you hurt? Do they need a nurse to help out in the church? Ted!" she screamed. "Answer me, please!"

Ted turned his head slowly and looked directly into Tracy's eyes.The expression on his face was one of disbelief. Suddenly, his eyes began filling with tears. He sobbed as he spoke. "Tracy, we had trouble finding Ralph Wilson in the church. His body was blown to bits. I found his hand, still clutching the doorknob on the confessional door."He choked up, then continued speaking: "Ralph's finger still carried the ring that his wife and kids gave him for his birthday. That was the only way I could identify him -- !"

"What happened in there?" she asked sobbing, still clutching Ted's hand.

"Someone attached a bomb to the confessional door. Ralph was the only one searching on that side of the church. When he opened the confessional door to see if anyone was hiding inside, he activated the bomb - and - and it exploded! Tracy, they still hadn't found his head when I left." Ted hesitated a moment and wiped his eyes. "That should have been *me* inside of that church tonight. Ralph worked the shift for me. That should be me lying in that church - Not Ralph!" he shouted, pounding the dashboard of the car with his closed fist.

A moment later, Ted covered his face with both his hands and began to weep like a small child at his mother's side. Tracy helped Ted to slide over to the passenger seat. She drove to Christian Hospital, hoping to get him something to quiet him down for the rest of the night.

CHAPTER XIV

Ted Namsky hit the medical rolls. His nerves needed time to settle down. He didn't see much of Tracy in the weeks that followed. He was jumpy - on edge all the time and he didn't want her to see him in the state he was in. Ted felt that a change might be good for him. To get away from the beat car for awhile.

A new unit was being formed. Its purpose was to provide police protection for the EL train passengers in the city. In the passing months, numerous outbreaks of robberies, muggings and thefts had occurred on both the trains and on the station platforms.

Ted had decided to join this new unit. He volunteered to give it a try for thirty days. He chose the 6:30 p.m. to 2:30 a.m. shift, which was known as the *power watch*. Besides asking for the late tour of duty, he also requested working the worst crime-riddled stations on the line. He put his request in and got what he asked for.

The first roll call in a new unit is always the roughest. New faces. New methods of working. New regulations. There was always something new and different to learn.

Ted reported to his new unit at 6:00 p.m. sharp. He received his working instructions and his two-way radio, which was his only link with the police department. Once he was on that train, he was on his own!

Ted stood on the station platform, slowly digesting the location. The south bound train had finally arrived. This was the tail end of rush hour traffic and the cars were carrying eighty percent capacity per car. The train stopped to pick up and drop off passengers. Ted boarded the train and walked directly to the conductor's booth in the car. He rested his back against the wall and scanned his eyes slowly over the other passengers. All eyes were focused on him! He could feel an atmosphere of hatred for policemen, slowly burrowing into him. He knew this was a rough assignment, but the reality of what was happening shocked him. Looking at people from a squad car as you passed by was a lot different from having them sitting and staring at you and not be able to get away from their staring. He wanted to crawl under a seat, just to get away from those staring eyes. He suddenly realized that he was the only Caucasian in the entire train car.

The end of the line finally arrived. This was it - his station to guard for the next eight hours. This was to be his domain. This was what he gave up the beat car for.

His duties were fairly simple: keep the loiterers and panhandlers off the platform, away from the cashier's cage; in fact, out of the station completely. He had to keep an eye out for potential pickpockets, muggers and purse snatchers. He also had to check the cashier's cage on the half-hour to make sure that everything was all right.

It was on his third night of duty, in the new unit, that Ted got the hell scared out of him. While he was talking with the cashier, the warning light of an approaching train, that was mounted on the ceiling, flashed *ON* and *OFF*. As the train came to a stop, four loud explosions rang out, simultaneously.

Ted ran up two flights of stairs - two steps at a time. With his revolver drawn, he was ready for the worst. It wasn't unusual for a patron, waiting on the platform, to be shot by someone riding in a passing train. That was the thought that kept running through Ted's mind as he ran up the stairs --had someone been shot?

As Ted came within eye level of the platform, he saw three young boys sprawled out on the platform, facing downward. The oldest boy couldn't have been more than twelve.

"My God. They're shot!" he shouted to himself. One of the boys lifted his head, smiled and looked directly at Ted. The young boy whispered something to one of the other boys and they all stood up. The oldest boy picked up a brown paper sack and tried to hide it behind his back. They started to move towards the opposite end of the platform.

"Hold it right there!" Ted ordered, putting his service revolver back into his holster. "What's going on here?"

"I saw it all, Officer," said an elderly woman who was resting her aged body on a wooden bench. "Those three boys climbed up on that roof, over there, and then climbed up on the platform. That tall boy took something out of the paper bag, that he's got hidden behind his back, and placed it on the train tracks. When the train pulled into the station, where were several loud *'Bangs'*. The boys pretended that they were shot and laid down on the platform."

"Come over here!" Ted shouted angrily, pointing to the oldest boy. "Bring that bag over here to me."

"Yes, Sir, Officer,"responded the boy as he walked towards Ted Namsky. He handed him the bag, Ted opened the bag and looked inside. It contained a couple dozen railroad signaling torpedoes. They were used to warn trains when there was danger ahead.

"Thank God that's all it was," Ted whispered to himself. "Lincoln-244," he said into his two-way radio.

"Lincoln Headquarters."answered the special dispatcher. "Go ahead Lincoln-244."

"I've got three youths for the juvenile officers. They were popping railroad torpedoes on the train tracks. Send me a beat car to transport them to the district station."

"Ten-four - Lincoln-244. They're on their way," said the dispatcher.

"O.K. boys, let's go downstairs and wait for your transportation," said Ted as he escorted the three boys down the stairway.

The rest of the week was relatively quiet. It was the second week that proved to be a little bit more exciting.

It started out as a normal Saturday night with its regular problems of drunks and panhandlers. Ted walked the EL platform, checking the tops of buildings next to and across the street from the platform. A shade shot up in a window, in a building, that he was standing adjacent too.

From the looks, Ted guessed it was a bedroom. The light was on. A pretty women of about twenty-eight walked into the room with her back facing the window. She removed her blouse, and then her skirt. She lit up a cigarette - clad in only her bra and panties,

Hey, this ain't to bad, Ted thought to himself, and she's pretty too. The young woman turned and saw Ted watching her. She sat on the edge of the bed and slowly removed her shoes and stockings, occasionally looking up at the window. She stood up and removed her bra and stretched her arms up in the air. She put her cigarette in a ashtray, on a small table next to the bed, and started to remove her panties. She pulled them below her bellybutton and then stopped - walked over to the window, smiled at Ted, waved her hand in a friendly greeting and then pulled the shade down.

"Shucks!" Ted said aloud. He looked at his watch. Five after twelve. The moon was bright - illuminating the entire area around the platform.

Thank God. Only two and a half hours to go, Ted thought to himself.

The noise of men's loud voices, coming from the street directly below him, quickly caught his attention. He leaned over the wooden guardrail and looked down into the street. two men were arguing in front of a tavern.

After a few moments of shouting, one man shoved the other, sending him tripping into the street directly in the path of an oncoming car. The blast from the automobile's horn sent the second man scurrying to his feet, trying to get out of the automobile's way. Dodging the car, the second man pulled a gun from his back pants pocket and began firing the gun wildly at the first man, who was standing on the sidewalk.

Everyone watching the fight ran for cover as the little metal bullets whizzed past them, striking the brick buildings. One of the tavern patrons fell to the ground, clutching his stomach with both hands. He lay on the sidewalk, groaning loudly. Within minutes there were men on both sides of the street shooting at each other.

"Lincoln-244!" Ted Namsky shouted into his two-way radio. No response. He repeated his call. "Emergency! Emergency! Lincoln Headquarters, this is Lincoln-244! Come in please!" Still no response came from his two-way radio. "Hey! Where the hell is everybody?" He shouted into the radio microphone. Still no response from the dispatcher.

The gunfire from the street below grew more intense. Two more men lay on the sidewalk - bleeding, motionless. From out of nowhere, a voice shouted, "Hey look. There's a honky on the EL platform!" Another voice shouted, "Get Him!"

All of a sudden, the men in the street below pointed their weapons toward the EL platform and began firing. Flashes of light! Puffs of smoke! Claps of thunder echoed off the brick walls of the buildings. The small lead bullets whizzed past Ted. One bullet struck the visor on his hat, lifting it off his head. The hat spun through the air, flew over the wooden guardrail and landed in the street below. Ted stepped back from the railing and ran over to a metal girder for protection. A bullet tore through the wooden floor boards, tearing a hole through his left shoe. The bullet only scraped Ted's big toe, but it made a hell of a hole on the top of his shoe.

"Emergency! Emergency!" Ted again shouted into his two-way radio. Still no response.

A voice from the street below screamed, "Someone get up on that platform and get him!"

"I'll go," a man volunteered. "Me too!" shouted another voice.

Ted began to panic. "Hey! Where the hell are you guys at?" he shouted into the two-way radio, pressing the on-off button, frantically. "Listen!" he continued, "if any of you assholes can hear me, I'm only going to get a chance to say this once! This is Lincoln-244. I'm at the Stony Island EL station. I'm up on the platform. There's a hell of a gun battle going on down in the street below me - and now everyone's coming after me!"

The sound of stamping feet came from the wooden stairs. Ted dropped his radio down on the platform and drew his gun. Two heads appeared coming up on the stairway.

"Hold it! Police officer!" Ted shouted, hoping his yell would startle and stop the two men from coming the rest of the way up. Both men took aim and fired at Ted. One bullet tore through the patch on the left shoulder of his jacket.

Ted pointed his revolver at the two men and fired - once - twice - three - four - five times. The two gunmen disappeared. Ted could hear them tumbling down the wooden stairs. He quickly reloaded his gun, ready for the next wave of intruders that wanted to get his scalp.

Suddenly, in the far off distance, he could hear the crying wail of oncoming police sirens. Ted began to breathe a little easier, now that he knew that help was coming. The danger still wasn't over. The screaming sirens faded out in the street directly below him. The sound of many stamping feet came from the wooden stairs - this made Ted hold his breathe again.

Do these guys want to kill me, too? Ted thought to himself. Were they trying to get away from the officers downstairs? Ted would be ready for them this time. He took careful aim at the stairway - and just waited. Within seconds, a policeman's hat came into view.

"Hold it, fella." the voice shouted. "We're police officers too!"

"If you are," Ted said, "come up slowly and show yourselves!"

A sergeant and a patrolman were the first ones up the stairway. Ted put his revolver back into his holster, fastening the leather safety strap.

"Who notified you?" Ted asked the sergeant.

"The girl in the cashier's cage downstairs called her supervisor when she heard all the shooting. She fainted when she saw the two men run into the lobby with guns. Her supervisor called our dispatchers and told them what was happening over here," explained the sergeant.

"I tried to reach the dispatcher several times on that piece of shit we call a radio, but the damn thing just wouldn't work,"said Ted.

"How was it working when you received it tonight?"asked the sergeant.

"It worked fine,"Ted answered. "When I first got to the El platform and checked in with the dispatcher, everything worked fine. Then, when the commotion started downstairs, I tried to reach the dispatcher, but couldn't get anything working on that fuckin' hunk of shit!"

The sergeant picked up the radio and examined it. He tried the on-off switch and pressed the signal button several times. Removing the back of the two-way radio, the sergeant said, "Know what your problem is, Officer?"

"What?" Ted asked.

"The damn battery went dead." The sergeant laughed.

"Great! That's just great!"replied Ted, throwing his arms up into the air in total disgust. "That's all I needed. Now my day is really complete!"

"Not quite," said the sergeant, smiling.

"What do you mean?" asked Ted.

"You've got at least four long hours of report writing ahead of you before you can go home and you'll have to explain how you broke the plastic case on the radio to the Captain!"

CHAPTER XV

Duty in the EL unit detail finally ended. Ted was transferred back to his original district. It felt good to be back in the district, riding the beat cars again.

Ted started the midnight shift on a Thursday. He couldn't believe his eyes the first night of roll call. The group of officers he was assigned to work with were the biggest bunch of goof-offs in the district. The sergeant called the men to attention. Two lines formed in front of the watch commander, who was conducting the roll call that night.

Ted was standing at attention in the center of the second line. The sergeant gave the *At Ease* command, then called off the officers names. At the end of the first line, two men leaned against an officer between them, so that he wouldn't fall down on the ground.

Ted looked down at the feet of the officer who was standing at attention in front of him. Ted laughed to himself. The officer was wearing two different color socks - one black and one brown. The officer standing next to Ted released a loud yawn. He looked as if he had just gotten out of bed. Ted also noticed that the officer's shoes were on the wrong feet. The man resembled a character from one of the old time movies.

Ted tapped the officer on his shoulder and remarked, "Excuse me, I don't mean to be rude, but don't your feet hurt?"

"Why do you ask, lad?" asked the older officer..

"Because, your shoes are on the wrong feet!" Ted answered, smiling.

"God-damn-it,. I did it again,"said the officer, laughing loudly. "Let me tell you, lad,"he continued as he took off his shoes. "I always buy my shoes a half size larger because of how bad my feet swell up. The shoes are comfortable that way. When I work the midnight watch, I'm always so damn tired that half the time I don't realize that I'm putting the wrong shoes on the wrong feet. Thanks for telling me, lad."

Ted smiled as the sergeant called the men to attention again. Ted's partner for the night was the officer whose shoes had been on the wrong feet.

The squad cars began moving out of the station parking lot. Some men went directly on patrol, while others pulled into the station garage for a gas and oil check.

"How about you driving tonight, lad?" asked Ted's partner, handing him the keys for the shiny new squad car. "I'm really bushed. If it remains quiet for a couple of hours, I'll be able to catch a few winks, that is, if it's O.K. with you?"

"Sure, it's O.K." said Ted as he took the keys and got into the squad car. The aging officer sat down in the passenger's seat.

"By the way, lad," said the officer, "my name's Andy - Andy Corkel."

"Ted - Ted Namsky." Ted replied, shaking his new partner's hand.

"Just take it easy, lad. Don't speed and don't get overly anxious to make pinches," said Andy. "I'm up for my pension in a couple of months and I don't aim to get killed now and have the city screw me out of the pension. Just do what I tell you and we'll get along fine, lad. Now tell me, just how long have you been working the streets?"

"About eight months," Ted answered. He started the squad car.

"Just as I thought," laughed Andy. "You're a cherry! Still a rookie." Andy slouched down in his seat and closed his weary eyes.

"How long have you been on the force, Andy?" asked Ted.

"Thirty-five years, lad. Thirty-five long, hard and rough years."

Ted picked up the microphone. "Car-2212. We're up and running on the streets."

"Ten-four - 2212." answered the dispatcher.

Ted turned to talk to his partner, but Andy was fast asleep, snoring louder than the calls coming in over the car radio speaker. Ted smiled as he drove the squad car to its assigned area of patrol.

A black 1967 four-door Oldsmobile sped down 71st Avenue at a high rate of speed. Officer Namsky was waiting at a stoplight when the black car sped through the intersection, hitting a staggering pedestrian, sending him flying up into the air.

The black Olds continued onward without stopping. Ted switched on the Mars lights and siren. A squad car coming in the opposite direction stopped to help the man lying in the street.

Ted signaled to the driver of the other squad car that he was going after the black Olds. Ted's foot tromped down on the gas pedal. The squad car turned the corner on two wheels. Within minutes, Ted was in close pursuit behind the speeding black Oldsmobile.

Ted's squad car hit a deep pot hole in the street. Andy Corkel's hat flew off his head, landing on the rear seat. Andy woke up, startled! He looked out the side window, only to see the landscape whizzing past him. He leaned over and looked at the speedometer. The red needle was resting on the ninety mark.

"Holy Lord! May all the good saints in heaven protect us!" screamed Andy. "Just what in the hell are you trying to do to us, lad? Kill us both?"

"That black Olds up ahead of us just hit a guy and took off," Ted shouted, manipulating the steering wheel from side to side. "Contact the dispatcher and let him know what we've got going."

Andy grabbed the microphone. "Car - 2212." he shouted.

"Go ahead, 2212." answered the dispatcher.

"Keep the line open," Officer Corkel continued. "We're in pursuit of a hit- and- run suspect."

"All cars stand by," said the dispatcher. "2212 is now in pursuit of a hit-and-run suspect. Go ahead, 2212. The lines are open. Give us your directions."

"What damn street are we on, lad?" Andy shouted.

"We're on 71st Avenue heading west, just passing Montclair Avenue," Ted answered. "That son-of-a-bitch is going to try and make a run for the suburbs. If he gets past Cicero Avenue we'll lose him!"

"We're on 71st Avenue heading west. We just passed Montclair Avenue," said Andy into the microphone. "We're chasing a black..." Andy hesitated. "Just what in the hell are we chasing, lad?" he asked.

"A 1967 black four-door Oldsmobile," Ted answered jerkily as the squad car hit another pot hole.

"A black, 1967, four-door Oldsmobile," Andy continued. "Looks like the suspect is making a run for the suburbs. Request you set up some road blocks to stop him."

"Ten-four," answered the dispatcher. "Stay in pursuit and notify us of any change in his direction. Don't lose him!"

"Don't lose him!" Andy shouted into the microphone. "*MOTHER MARY!* It's a good thing this squad car doesn't have wings or this damn fool driving it would be swooping down on that suspect car like an eagle catching a field mouse!"

Andy looked up at the roof of the squad car and said, "Saint Peter, get ready to open those golden gates, 'cause this fool's gonna get me up there in front of you before this night is over!"

Ted laughed, but Andy Corkel wasn't laughing - he was sweating!.

The black Olds made a quick right turn. As they made their turn, the right front tire blew. The black car hit a metal waste basket resting on the sidewalk at the corner. The car finally came to rest inside a grocery store. It entered the store through the large plate glass window.

Ted stopped the squad car, got out and ran over to the damaged car. He dragged the two occupants out onto the sidewalk. Andy remained inside the squad car, He couldn't move. After that high speed chase, his feet felt like rubber bands, that were about ready to snap.

"They're just kids," Ted shouted, "not more than fifteen years old. Call for a squadrol and we'll get them to a hospital. Run a check on the car plates and see if they're hot."

Andy dropped the microphone twice before he finally conveyed Ted's message to the dispatcher....

The interrogation room in the police station was empty when Ted Namsky and Andy Corkel arrived. Shortly afterwards, the squadrol officers brought the two teenagers back from the hospital.

"How are they?" Ted asked.

"They're all right," answered the heaviest of the two squadrol officers. "They're bruised up a little, but the Doc at the hospital says that they'll live."

"Sit down over here," Ted insisted, pointing at two empty chairs in the far corner of the room. The two boys did as they were told without uttering a single word.

The beat sergeant entered the interrogation room, followed by two youth officers. Following an hour of paper work, the youth officers took custody of the two juveniles.

"O.K., Namsky and Corkel," said the beat sergeant, "get back on your beat patrol."

"Not me, Sarge!" said Andy. "It'll take the miracle of Saint Gabriel coming down from the heavens above, blowing his golden trumpet before I'll get back in a squad car with that maniac," he shouted, waving his finger in Ted's face. "The Good Saints preserve us." Andy continued. " He almost killed us in that squad car. Ninety miles an hour, he was going - he was! No, sir, Sergeant, I won't ride with that lad anymore."

The Sergeant turned, facing Ted. Ted shrugged his shoulders, remarking, "I had to catch them Sarge, didn't I?"

"Step outside for a few minutes, Namsky," replied the sergeant, "I want to have a talk with Andy."

Ten minutes had passed when the interrogation room door finally opened.

"Andy will ride with you, Namsky, provided you're a little more cautious with your driving habits," said the sergeant, smiling.

"O.K., Sarge, I promise," said Ted. "Come on, Andy, let's get back on patrol."

"You go out to the squad car, lad. I'll be out in a few minutes," said Officer Corkel as he turned and started walking up the stairs that led to the roll call and locker rooms.

"Hey! Where're you going, Andy?" asked Ted.

Andy stopped, hesitated a moment, then turned around slowly and looked down towards Ted and the sergeant. "I've got to change my trousers, lad," he replied. "The brown stain won't blend in with this lovely blue material that I'm wearing." Andy turned around and continued walking up the stairway as Ted Namsky and the beat sergeant fought desperately with themselves, not to burst out laughing.

Saturday night was here again with the same old problems. It seemed as though every weekend, people wanted to kill each other.

"Car 2212!" paged the dispatcher.

Ted picked up the microphone. "2212," he replied.

"2212, see the complainant, a Mister Sam Williams, at 3617 South Corton Street. He has information for the police about suspicious happenings in his building."

"Ten-four, squad!" said Ted.

"3617 South Corton," interrupted Andy. "That'll be the project buildings, wouldn't it, lad?"

"That's right, Andy," Ted answered.

Both men remained silent until they were within a block of their destination. It wasn't unusual to receive a phony call, but a call from the projects sometimes meant a possible ambush.

Andy parked the squad car at the alley entrance, in back of the project buildings.

"Lad," he said, looking at Ted, "you've got to be careful around here. Take it from this old timer, never stand in open light where you'll make a good target. If you're not sure of the area, stay in the shadows until you feel that everything's all right. *Then* proceed."

The two officers exited the squad car. Officer Corkel quickly took a survey of the surrounding area, looking for silent movements in the hidden shadows. Satisfied that everything looked all right, they proceeded to the entrance doors of the large building. Ted tried the doors. They were locked.

"We'll have to use the back entrance, Andy."

"Go ahead, lad. I'll be right behind you, but make sure you keep a sharp eye for any unusual movements."

The two officers followed the short sidewalk leading to the back entrance of the building. Ted tugged at the doors. They were locked too.

"I don't like this, lad! I don't like this at all!" said Andy. He nervously surveyed the area again.

"Come on, lad, let's get out of here," he shouted, pulling at Ted's arm.

A loud scraping noise came from above their heads. Both officers looked up, just in time to see a large metal refrigerator being pushed over a small balcony.

The refrigerator fell freely from the fifteenth floor of the building, dropping straight toward both officers.

"Run your fool ass off, lad, and be making it quick!" yelled Andy, still pulling at Ted's arm. He yanked Ted out of the way of the falling refrigerator -- just in the nick of time.

The metal refrigerator buried half of itself into the asphalt pavement. Metal chips and rock particles shot in every direction. The small metal objects ricocheted off the building and garbage cans, like wild searching bullets. A piece of stone found its way into Ted's neck. Blood flowed down onto his shirt and leather jacket.

"Are you all right, lad?" Andy asked.

"I'm O.K., Andy." Ted wiped some of the blood away from the wound with his handkerchief. Looking over the demolished scraps of metal lying on the pavement, Ted remarked, "Goddamn, Andy, that could have been us lying under that heap of metal."

"I know, lad, now let's quickly be moving our asses out of here!"

A bright flash appeared above them, followed by a loud explosion that echoed throughout the alley. A small metal projectile brought Andy down, just before they reached their squad car. Ted dragged his partner over to an area that was free of any further attack on them. Ted knelt down, next to his partner, slightly lifting his head.

"Where did you get hit, Andy?" he asked anxiously.

"In me back, lad. In me back," Andy whispered, just before he passed out.

Several more shots rang out. The small bullets hit the ground, narrowly missing Ted and his wounded partner. Ted made his way back to their squad car, grabbed the microphone and called for help. Within minutes, the street was swarming with squad cars and police officers.

The shooting had ceased with the approach of the first assist car. The would-be assassins had made their getaway. The two injured officers were transported to Christian Hospital for medical attention.

The emergency room was filled to capacity as they rolled Andy Corkel, lying on a stretcher, through the large double doors. Ted walked behind the stretcher, holding his handkerchief over the wound in his neck.

Tracy Tate was treating a wound on a young boy's forehead, when she saw the group of officers coming into the emergency room.

"Ted!" she screamed as she ran towards him. "What happened? Are you hurt bad? Let me see the wound. What happened to the other officer?"

"It was a setup, Tracy." Ted answered softly. "They were waiting for us and they shot my partner in the back."

Following a brief examination by the doctor on duty, two interns wheeled Andy Corkel's stretcher onto an elevator. Ted walked towards the elevator. "I'll see you later, Tracy, O.K.? I'm going up with Andy now."

One of the interns stopped him before he could get onto the elevator. "Sorry, Officer," he said. "Your partner's got to make this trip on his own. Get your wound attended to and say..." The intern hesitated for a moment. "Say a little prayer for him."

The elevator doors closed. Ted watched the little circles light up, one at a time, above the elevator door. When the last number lit up, he knew that Andy had reached the operating floor. Tracy tugged at Ted's arm. "Come with me ,Ted. I'll take care of that cut,"she insisted.

Ted followed her into a cubical, without saying a word. He sat himself down on a small metal stool, watching Tracy gather iodine, cotton swabs, cloth and tape from one of the white metal cabinets hanging on the wall.

"How have you been, Tracy?" he asked as she removed the bloody handkerchief from the wound.

"I'm fine,"she replied, looking straight into his eyes as she spoke. "Why haven't you gotten in touch with me since the night of Officer Wilson's terrible accident?" she asked.

He couldn't look up into her face anymore, so he looked down at the small ceramic squares on the floor and replied, "I couldn't, Tracy. I needed more time to think. I needed to be alone. I had to have time to find myself. I didn't think that you wanted to see me again, not after turning down my marriage proposal. The department put together a new unit to protect the EL passengers. That's where I've been working for awhile. I just returned to the district last Thursday.

Tracy placed her finger tips under his chin and lifted it up - slowly. Their eyes met. "Ted," she paused... "You know that I love you. Just how much, I wasn't really sure of, until I saw you walk through those doors tonight. When I saw you, I knew then - just *how much.*" Her eyes filled with tears as she bent over and kissed him gently on his lips.

"Ask me that special question again - *now.*" she whispered softly.

"Will you marry me?" he said.

"Yes - yes!" she answered immediately, kissing him gently again.

Ted flinched when the softness of her cheek brushed against the wound on his neck.

"I'm sorry," she whispered, taking a piece of alcohol soaked cotton to cleanse the wound....

Officer Namsky sat in a leather bound chair, in the hospital outer lobby, puffing on a cigarette as he anxiously awaited the results of his partner's operation. Two detectives questioned him between the drags that he took from his cigarette. Other policemen nervously paced the floor, eager to give their blood, if Andy Corkel needed it.

A doctor, still dressed in his blood stained operating clothes, came into the lobby. Tracy Tate's tour was over and she sat at Ted's side, waiting to hear the news of Andy Corkel's operation.

"Gentlemen," the doctor began, "he's going to make it! He'll be a very sick man for a long time, but eventually, he'll be all right. We had to remove his left kidney. The bullet tore it apart. It was totally useless to him."

Ted let out a deep sigh of relief as he tightly held onto Tracy's hand.

"Are you off duty yet, Ted?" she asked. She rummaged through her purse, finally locating a set of car keys.

"I've got about two hours of paper work ahead of me," he answered, putting out his cigarette. "When I finish, I'll be through for the night."

"Did you drive to work tonight?" she asked.

"No, not tonight. I rode down with one of the other officers. I'll catch a cab when I'm ready to go home. Why do you ask?"

"I finally got my driver's license and bought a car two weeks ago," she answered, happily.

"No kidding, Tracy? You're driving now? Say, you're getting up in this world," he said, smiling.

"Aren't I though?" she replied. "I'll meet you at the station and I'll drive you home tonight."

"It'll take too long," he insisted.

"I'll wait," she protested, "besides, we've a lot to talk about on the way home!"

CHAPTER XVI

A light misty rain fell on the squadrol's windshield, blocking out everything from view. Officer Leon Bukowski turned on the windshield wipers.

"Nice to be working together again, Ted, isn't it?" he asked.

"Sure is," Ted replied as he was writing some notes down on a piece of paper on his clipboard.

"Have you heard how Andy's doing?" asked Leon.

"I was just up to the hospital to see him, Leon. Andy's doing fine. It's only been a week since he was shot and already he wants to get out of bed and go to work."

"Well, that's a good sign anyway," said Leon. "You can't keep a stubborn bull like him down on his back."

"No, you can't." Ted laughed as he wrote.

Officer Bukowski made a right turn at the corner of 35th and Scott Street, heading west bound on 35th Street.

"What time have you got, Ted?" asked his partner. "My damn watch stopped again."

"One thirty-five a.m.," Ted answered, sounding bored. "Boy, with this rain we're going to have a slow night."

Leon laughed. "Don't knock it, pal. Don't knock it. Hey, look under that street light on the corner. See those two crazy dressed girls standing there?" Leon pointed towards the girls.

"Yeah, I see them," Ted answered. "You think they're a couple of hookers?"

"Could be." Leon replied. "I've never seen those two working this district before. Let's check them out."

The squadrol stopped in front of the two young women. Both girls were dressed in oversized, multicolored rain coats. One girl's arm was around the other girl's waist, as she rested her head on her girlfriend's shoulder. Officer Namsky got out of the squadrol and walked towards the two women.

"Why are you two girls standing in the rain, on this corner, at one-thirty in the morning?" he asked, using a tone of authority in his voice.

"Please help us, Officer!" pleaded the taller of the two women. "My friend here doesn't feel too well. We were waiting for either a cab, or bus. I have to get her to a hospital."

"Hey, Leon," Ted shouted, "come on out and give me a hand."

Leon stuck his head out of the squadrol's window. "What's the matter?" he asked.

"Got a sick girl over here. Help me get her into the back of the squadrol. We're only a few blocks from Wilson Memorial Hospital." Ted turned towards the sick girl. "Miss, we'll have you and your friend at the hospital in no time."

The two officers helped the two women into the back of the squadrol, then got into the cab of the truck.

"2271," said Ted Namsky.

"Go ahead, 2271," said the dispatcher.

"Picked up a couple of sick women on 35th and Segal. We're gonna transport them over to Wilson memorial Hospital."

"Ten-four!" replied the dispatcher.

Five minutes later they were pulling into the emergency entrance to Wilson Memorial. Ted helped the ill young woman into one of the examining rooms, then went back to talk with her girlfriend.

After Ted jotted down some notes in his notebook, the two officers were ready to leave the hospital and go back on patrol. The doctor came out of the examining room just as the two officers were ready to leave.

"Just a minute, Officers," he said. "Where do you think you're going?"

"Back on patrol." Leon replied. "Why?"

"Oh no you're not!" said the doctor.

"What do you mean, we're not?" interrupted Ted Namsky.

"That woman you just brought in here..." the doctor hesitated.

"Yeah, what about her?" asked Leon.

"She's pregnant," continued the doctor.

"So what! shouted Leon. "Neither one of us is the damn father! You're the doctor. Take care of her."

"That girl is ready to have her baby," the doctor continued, ignoring Leon's comments. "I've given her some medication to ease the pain. She has no means of support. No money! No hospitalization! She has to be transported to County Hospital and as long as you're here there's no need for me to call for a squadrol to take her there. Her labor pains are about ten minutes apart. If you hurry, you should make it to County just in time for the big event.

"Holy Jesus - Mary - and Joseph!" Leon slapped himself on his forehead with the palm of his hand. "What in the hell did we get ourselves into now?"

The young woman walked slowly out of the examining room. Her face revealed her discomfort with each step that she took. Ted grabbed her by the elbow and rushed her towards the exit doors. "Let's get going!" he shouted to his partner.

The pregnant woman and her girlfriend were put into the back of the squadrol again.

"One of us should be riding in back with them. Have you had any experience delivering a baby, Leon?" Ted asked.

"Nope!" Leon replied instantly.

"Neither have I," said Ted. "Do you want to ride back there with her?"

"Nope!" came the same reply from Officer Bukowski.

"O.K., I'll do it." said Ted. "No sense in us standing out here arguing. You drive. Take the expressway, but take it easy. Riding in the back of this thing is like being on a roller coaster."

Officer Namsky crawled up into the back of the squadrol, shutting the door behind him. His partner got into the cab and slid back the small door on the back of the cab so he could talk with Ted.

The pregnant woman shifted nervously, back and forth, on the wooden bench. The squadrol began to move forward.

"Can make a suggestion, Miss?" asked Ted. "There's a set of metal rings just above your head. You'd better hold onto them so you don't slide off of the seat."

The woman took Ted's advice. As she grabbed the metal rings, she let out a loud, sharp cry of pain, biting her bottom lip so hard, that it started to bleed.

"Holy cow!" shouted Ted. "Hey Leon! You'd better get this tin can rolling! I don't think we have to much Goddamn time left!"

"Right," Leon answered as the squadrol began to sway from side to side.

"We're coming to the expressway now, Ted," Leon shouted as the squadrol made a sharp left turn.

Ted slid off the seat and landed on the floor - feeling very embarrassed. He picked himself up and brushed himself off. Smiling, he said, "I guess I should have held onto those rings, too."

The squadrol hit a large pothole. The three occupants in the back almost touched the ceiling with the tops of their heads.

"Sorry about that, " Leon shouted, seeing his partner getting up off the floor again. The pregnant woman screamed in pain once more.

"I can't make it! I can't make it!" she repeated. "I can feel the baby starting to drop! Let me lay down - *PLEASE*! " she screamed.

"How much farther have we got to go?" shouted Ted.

"About a mile, Ted. Just one more mile to go."

"She's not going to make it, Leon!" Ted yelled as he removed a woolen blanket from the bench that he was sitting on. He wrapped the blanket around each of his arms; making a small sling.

"We're off the expressway, Ted. Only two more blocks to go. Tell her to hold on for a few more minutes. We'll make it!

"It's coming out!"screamed the woman, frantically. "I can feel it coming out right now! Oh God , please help me!" Large drops of perspiration formed on her forehead. Ted felt a squeamish churning starting inside his stomach. He was praying that she would listen to him and do what he said. He had to be firm with her. This was no time to be polite.

"Slide your ass to the end of that bench!" he ordered. The young woman obeyed him without hesitation. "Now spread your legs apart and set them up on the bench that I'm sitting on, " he continued. The girl followed his instructions. "Lift up her dress and coat," he shouted to the other girl.

She's not wearing any underpants, Ted thought, good! "Hey Leon, I can see the baby's head. It's starting to come out!"

"Don't you worry, pal,"laughed Officer Bukowski, "the hospital is coming right up."

Just before entering the hospital parking lot, the squadrol hit a deep dip in the street. *Ohhhhhhhhhhhhhhhh*! screamed the woman as the tiny baby fought its way into the outside world. Ted caught the baby in his makeshift blanket sling. The back of the squadrol was covered with a mixture of water and blood. And - of course - so was Officer Namsky's entire uniform.

The squadrol stopped in front of the hospital's emergency entrance. Leon hurried to the back of the squadrol. just as he opened the large door, the newborn baby began to cry.

"Welcome to this crazy world, kid, " Leon shouted

Nurses and interns came out from the hospital and took the mother and new baby inside on a stretcher. Leon lit up a cigar, smiled and said, "Here's to Ted Namsky. The new midwife of the 22nd District!"

"Screw you, Bukowski. Just drive me home so I can put a clean uniform on my back," said Ted.

Ted really felt good about completing his midwife chores.

CHAPTER XVII

Ted had just begun to brush his teeth when he heard a car honking from the street below. Sticking his head out the living room window, he saw that it was Tracy in her car, who was making all of the racket.

"Be down in a minute, Tracy," he shouted.

"Hurry up or I'll be late for work,"she said.

He quickly finished brushing his teeth and combed his hair. Fastening his utility belt, which held his holster and revolver, handcuffs, and other accessories, he hurried down the hallway stairs. Getting into the car, he gave Tracy a quick kiss on her lips.

"That's not much of a kiss after waiting so long for you, " she said, jokingly.

"Hurry! Just drive,"Ted laughed. "I'll make it up to you after we finish work tonight."

"Tell me, Ted, is it my mind, my personality, my looks or my body that makes you love me so much?" she asked, trying to put Ted on the spot.

He patted her thigh gently, saying, "Just keep driving. I'll give you that answer the next time that we're alone."

Just before reaching the police station, Ted threw a quick question at Tracy. "Tracy,"he paused, "a new tactical unit is being formed. They're asking for volunteers. It'll mean working in plainclothes and I won't have to be answering all of those domestic calls. The only drawback is that I'll be spending a lot of time in court with the arrests I make. I'd like to volunteer for the assignment. What do you think about the idea?"

"Do you really want to try for it, Ted? "she asked.

"Yes, I would, Tracy."

"Then do it!" she said without hesitation. "Get it out of your system now. When we're married next year, I'd like you to spend a little more time with me. Maybe by then, you'll find a spot where you'll be working straight days with the weekends off."

"Fat chance of that." he laughed. It'll be a long time before I can latch onto anything like that."

"I know," she answered, smiling, "I was just wishing out loud, Ted - that's all. Here's the station. See you later."

"See you," he answered, giving Tracy another quick kiss as he got out of her car.

The traffic light turned green. The squad car moved along lazily through the intersection.

"2217 is up and clear, squad," said Ted into the microphone.

"Ten-four, 2217." answered the dispatcher.

Leon Bukowski looked at his partner. "Did you see Tracy tonight, Ted?" he asked. As Leon spoke, he quickly turned the steering wheel to avoid hitting a pothole.

"Yeah, I saw her. She drove me to the station tonight."

Did you tell her about the new unit that's being out together?"

"I told her." Ted shifted his weight on the car seat, trying to find a comfortable position.

"Well? What did she think about you trying out for it?"

"She told me to do what I thought was best for me," Ted replied, smiling.

"Great!" said Leon. "When we finish our tour tonight, let's talk with the Captain together, O.K.?"

"Sure. Sure." Ted laughed. "Whatever you say, Leon."

The squad car traveled south bound on Western Avenue.

"2217." blared the radio speaker.

"2217." Ted answered.

"2217, a woman calling for help at 50th and Western Avenues." said the dispatcher.

"We're on our way, squad." Ted turned on the Mars lights and switched on the siren. Officer Bukowski pushed his foot down on the gas pedal.

Three squad cars were already at the scene when car 2217 arrived. A sergeant, lieutenant and three beat patrolmen were talking to an elderly woman. Officer Bukowski stopped the squad car and remained inside while his partner went over to investigate the complaint.

"What've you got, Sarge?" Ted asked, taking out a pen and pocket notebook.

"Hi, Namsky," replied the sergeant. "Have you got the paper on this one?"

"Yep," Ted replied. "The dispatcher just assigned it to us."

"As far as I can figure out," the sergeant continued, "this woman was on her way to work. She's a night cleaning woman at one of the hotels downtown. Just as she was passing the alley, a hand reached out from behind a telephone pole, grabbed her around the neck and dragged her into the alley. The arm tightened around her throat - choking her. Then, she said that she felt a cold piece of metal press against her neck. A man's voice said,"Mama! This is a stick up! I've got a gun pointed at your neck. Don't give me no kind of trouble. Just drop your bag on the ground and walk away quietly, in the opposite direction - and keep your mouth shut! I don't wants ta hurt you, Mama. I just wants your bread." The old woman got mad and wasn't about to hand over her purse to her assailant.

"She kicked him in the shin bone with the heel of her shoe, hit him in the stomach with her right elbow and grabbed his testicles with her left hand. I would say that she took the guy by surprise, because he immediately released his grip on her throat. She spun around and gave this guy a karate chop on his wrist. He dropped the gun. While he was hopping around in pain, she picked up his gun, closed her eyes, pointed the gun in his direction and began firing at him! She got off four shots before she heard him scream. She said he ran down the street, got into a car and drove away. He probably had the car stashed there, ready for a quick getaway. Anyhow, when it was all over, she panicked, threw away the gun and started screaming. We haven't found the gun yet."

One of the searching officers shouted, "Here's the gun, Sarge. Over here - under this car." The officer picked up the gun and brought it to the sergeant. The chrome plated .25 caliber automatic glistened under the street light, as it rested in the sergeant's hand. He sniffed the end of the barrel.

"This is probably the weapon she used. It's been fired recently." said the sergeant. "Namsky, take the woman with you and cruise around the area. Maybe you'll get lucky and she'll spot him walking on the street. From the looks of those drops of blood, he's hurt bad and isn't gonna drive too far in his condition."

"Right, Sarge," answered Ted, leading the elderly woman by her arm. "Come with me, Ma. We'll try to find that mean culprit."

At first, the old woman was reluctant to go with Officer Namsky, but she finally gave in and got into the squad car.

Leon was quickly briefed on the situation. The two officers and the elderly victim began their slow, tedious search of the surrounding area.

A half hour had passed - with no luck locating the suspect. The dispatcher broadcasted a report that there was a injured man at Christian Hospital. The man was supposedly shot in the leg during a robbery attempt. The alleged assailant had fled the crime scene and gotten away. Ted looked at Leon. "Hey," he said, "what do you think, Leon? Could be the guy we're looking for."

"I don't know,"replied Leon. "It could be him. It's a long shot, but what the hell, let's give it a shot. What have we got to lose? Let's go take a look at him."

"Car, 2217." said Ted Namsky into the microphone.

"Go ahead, 2217."

"Have the field lieutenant meet us at Christian Hospital. We're gonna have our victim take a look at your shooting victim."

"Ten-four, 2217," replied the dispatcher.

When the squad car entered the hospital parking lot, the field lieutenant was already there, standing at the doorway, waiting for them.

"What do you want to see me about, Namsky?" asked the lieutenant as he walked towards Ted.

"It's a long shot, *Lieut*, but we think that the injured guy in the hospital from the robbery attempt could actually be the same guy we're looking for. How about letting the old woman take a look at him?"

"I don't know,Ted,"said the lieutenant, scratching the back of his head. "We should conduct a proper lineup for her to view him. If it is the guy you're looking for, I'd like to nail him for it and put him away."

"How bad is he hurt?" asked Officer Bukowski.

"He's got a small caliber bullet in the left thigh and in his right shoulder. The last time I checked, the doctor was almost finished removing the lead slugs. They say that he'll be all right."

"Come on, how about it, Lieutenant?' Ted was almost pleading. "I've got that funny feeling that it's him."

"All right, Namsky," said the lieutenant, "just one quick look, but only for a moment. That's it!"

The elevator took the three officers and the old woman to the fourth floor of the hospital. They walked to the injured man's room.

"Remember, Namsky,"whispered the lieutenant, "just one quick look."

The lieutenant slowly opened the door. Everyone entered the sick man's room. The moment the old woman saw the injured man's face, she shouted, *THAT'S HIM*! That's the some-in-a-bitch that tried to take my money and made me miss a day of work! That's the some-in-a-bitch!" The old woman's voice was so loud that it startled the injured man, almost making him fall out of his bed.

"Give me your gun, Officer!"she begged the lieutenant. "I fix that no good some-in-a-bitch real good! You no need a trial when I fix him good!"

The lieutenant got red-faced and flustered when the old woman started tugging at his arm, pleading with him. Officers Namsky and Bukowski started to leave the room.

"And just where are you two going?" asked the lieutenant.

"Well, we sort of figured that you had the situation well in hand, Lieutenant, so we were going back on patrol," answered Leon, letting a burst of laughter slip out of his mouth.

"Take this woman down to the station," ordered the lieutenant, sternly. "And let her sign the complaint forms. Then , take her home!"

"Yes, sir!" said Ted, leading the old woman into the elevator, then out of the hospital.

"Boy, that was some tough old dame, wasn't she, Ted?" said Leon, laughing, as they both rode down Western Avenue.

"Sure was. I'm glad she wasn't mad at me."

The squad car stopped at an intersection for a red light. A slovenly dressed man staggered, as he walked on the sidewalk. He stopped and leaned up against a lamp post, right next to the squad car.

"Man, is he carrying a snout full," said Ted, pointing at the man. "Let's check him out."

The drunken man staggered towards the squad car, unzipped the front zipper of his pants and urinated on the door of the squad car - while singing loudly.

"Aw, shit!" shouted Ted, disgustedly. "Here we go again. Call for a wagon. I'll quiet his guy down."

It took less than a half hour for the squadrol to transport the drunken man back to the station, fill out the booking papers, turn the drunk over to the lockup keeper and go back on patrol.

Leon laughed loudly as they drove along their assigned beat.

"What's so damn funny?" asked Ted, not really able to keep a straight face himself.

"Could you," said Leon, tears in his eyes from laughing so hard, "imagine the expressions that we had on our faces when that drunk whipped it out and pissed all over our squad car door? If you really think about it, it's funny as hell!"

The dispatcher's voice broke into their conversation, "Car 2217."

"2217." Ted answered.

"Handle shots fired at 4721 west Toben Street."

"Ten-four, squad," Ted replied. "Hey Leon, we just passed that address not more than five minutes ago."

"Yes, I know." Leon made a quick "U" turn and turned the car around. He reached for the Mars light switch, but Ted stopped him.

"Forget the light and siren, Leon. We're too close for them. We'd scare anyone away if they heard us coming."

The blue and white squad car came to a screeching stop, fifty feet past the shooting address. It was a badly kept tavern.

Ted jumped out of the car, hid behind a lamp post for a short moment and quickly surveyed the entire area. The front construction of the tavern was half window and half brick wall. The brick wall rose to approximately five feet above the sidewalk.

In the center of a large plate glass window, just above the brick ledge, gaped a large hole. All of the lights inside the tavern were out. Officer Bukowski began to exit the squad car.

"Get the flashlights, Leon," Ted whispered. Stooping low, Ted ran over to the tavern wall, stopping just under the hole in the window. His partner ran to the lamp post and waited.

"Leon, shine your flashlight beam into the tavern. I want to take a quick look inside."

Officer Bukowski removed his revolver from his holster, turned on his flashlight and shined the beam of light into the tavern. Ted grabbed hold of the brick ledge, lifted himself up and peeked through the hole in the window. The end of a double-barreled shotgun was no more than three inches away from his face - *Click! Click!"*

The sound of the misfired weapon echoed inside Ted's head like a thousand explosions going off at one time. His legs felt like rubber as he fell to the sidewalk. A cold sweat quickly encased his entire body. Leon fired a shot into the tavern through the hole in the window.

"Come out with your hands up!" shouted Officer Bukowski, slowly pulling back the hammer on his revolver. He pointed his gun at the tavern doorway. "This is the police! I said to come out!" he ordered.

Within minutes, the street was jammed with squad cars. They covered the alley as well as the street.

"Don't shoot," said a quivering voice from inside the tavern. "Please hold your fire! Don't shoot no more! I give up! I'm coming out now!"

The field sergeant ran over to Leon. They waited together. Ted cocked his gun, pointing it at the doorway. Slowly, the tavern door opened. A thin, fragile looking old man of about seventy slowly exited through the doorway with his hands held high in the air.

"Don't shoot, Mister Policeman's!" the old man shouted. "Please don't shoots no more!"

"Well, I'll be Goddamned," said Leon, putting his revolver back into his holster. They walked over to the old man.

"Namsky, get on your radio and tell the dispatcher that we've got enough cars over here. Bukowski, go into the tavern and pick up any weapons that you find in there. I'll question the old man. He seems harmless enough," said the sergeant. "Right, Sarge," both officers answered as they headed for their given assignments.

Several minutes later, Ted walked back to the sergeant and old man. Leon came out of the tavern carrying a double-barreled shotgun in his hand. He looked at his partner, smiled, and threw two 12-gauge cartridge casings at him. Ted caught them and examined them carefully.

"Keep them as a souvenir, pal," said Leon. "Look at the primers on both of those cartridges. You'll see two firing pin indentations on each casing. You were real lucky, Ted! It's a good thing that guy is old and probably a little senile. He forgot to reload the shotgun when he aimed it at you!"

Ted found it hard to swallow. His mouth felt as if it were made of cotton. "What information did you get, Sarge?" he asked.

"He's nothing more than a cleaning man, Namsky," answered the sergeant. "After the tavern closed for the night, he began his cleaning choirs. Shortly after he started, he heard a noise coming from the front door. At first, he paid no attention to it. He thought it might be a drunk trying the door to see if the tavern was open. Well, the noises became louder. Suddenly, the small window in the center of the door was smashed to bits. A hand came through the small opening, trying to find the door lock , to open the door. The old man shouted at the suspect to go away or he'd call the police. Anyway, the old man said that the voice on the other side of the door told him that if he didn't open the door and let them in, they'd get in anyway and when they did, they would kill him!"

The sergeant took out a cigar, lit it, then continued talking. "The old man got scared, took the shotgun that the owner kept hidden behind the bar and pointed it towards the front of the tavern. He didn't aim the shotgun, just cocked it and fired! The lead pellets went through the plate glass window. The blast must have scared the hell out of the burglars, because they left right away. The guy that had his hand inside the tavern, through the small window, left half his jacket sleeve hanging on the jagged glass when he ran away.

"The old man was getting ready to call the police, when he heard another noise coming from below the hole in the plate glass window. He thought they were coming back to get him again. He picked up the shotgun and crept towards the window. He placed the front of the shotgun by the hole in the window, cocked it, and waited. Ted, when you looked through the hole, he thought you were one of the burglars. He panicked and pulled the triggers on the shotgun. When the gun didn't fire, he started backing away. He slipped and fell to the floor, just before Leon fired a round into the tavern. That's the whole story. Go back to the station and fill out your reports, and we'll finish things up here."

Ted walked back to the squad car and sat down. He placed both his hands on the steering wheel and started to think about what had just happened. The realization of just how close he had come to not having a head on his shoulders, hit him all at once. His hands began to shake - violently!

"Hey, Leon!" Ted shouted. His partner trotted back to the squad car, surprised by the sight of Ted sitting there - shaking uncontrollably.

"Will you do me a favor, Leon?" Ted asked.

"Sure, partner!" replied, Leon, smiling and understanding just what Ted's problem was. "What do you want me to do for you?"

"Drive this damn squad car back to the station for me. Right now, I don't think I can make it on my own!"

CHAPTER XVIII

Ted rested himself on the wooden bench inside of the squad room. All the other officers were dressed in uniform, except for him, he wore civilian street clothes.

This was the first night that the new district tactical unit was going into full operation. Officers Bukowski, Barner and Seccoro entered the squad room together. They also were dressed in civilian clothes. Upon seeing Ted sitting on the bench, they waved, walked over and sat down next to him.

"What's happening, Tim?" Ted asked as he got up to shake hands with him. "Long time no see! What've you been doing with yourself?"

"They've had me working on special details - school crossings, abandoned cars, directing traffic and serving warrants. Hell, Ted, they've had me doing a little bit of everything," answered Tim Barner. "Shit, when I heard they were forming this new unit, I jumped at the chance to get into it."

"Hey!"interrupted Leon,"isn't this great.The four of us will be working together. It's just like being back at the Academy."

"Yeah, it's super swell," said Tony Seccoro,yawning. "What in the hell time is it anyway? I forgot my wrist watch again."

Ted looked at his watch. "It's eleven-thirty, Tony."

"Shit, I should be back home in bed at this hour of the night,"he answered , yawning again.

"Whose home? And, whose bed are you referring to?"asked Leon, laughing. Everyone laughed at Leon's insinuation.

The captain entered the squad room. All the men formed ranks and stood at attention. Silence prevailed in the room. The captain inspected the men, took roll call and issued out the assignments. W hen the regular business was concluded, the captain spoke freely with the men.

"Men,"he began, taking out his pipe, filling it with tobacco and lighting it. He took a long drag and let out a small cloud of blue smoke that rose lazily towards the ceiling. "Tonight we're trying something new in the district. Officers Namsky, Bukowski, Seccoro and Barner are part of a special new tactical team. The crime rate in this district has risen tremendously, and the big brass downtown are screaming to high heaven about it. They want the crime rate statistics brought down. These officers will only be used for special assignments. They'll be free to move around the entire district. They can assist on some of the calls that are assigned to you. This is, of course, at their discretion. So be extra cautious! If you happen to see someone lurking in the shadows, it might very well be one of these officers."

One of the older officers spoke, interrupting the captain."Say, Captain," he began, "if we see someone sneaking around in the shadows, is it all right if we shoot him in the ass?" Everyone in the room, including the captain, laughed.

Officers Namsky, Bukowski, Barner and Seccoro sat red-faced and embarrassed as the officers in the room looked at them and continued laughing.

"Listen up, men,"continued the captain, being more serious."All kidding aside, be careful. Always make sure that you're not going to shoot another police officer by mistake." The captain paused a moment, then continued. "All right, that's it for now. Get to your assigned beats. The officers who are assigned to the hew tact unit, before you go out, stop by me office. I have a few more things to discuss with all of you. Everyone is dismissed."

The men gathered in clusters as they began leaving the squad room. The older officer, who had made the humorous remark, walked passed the tactical team officers. Suddenly he stopped, turned around and looked back at them. "*The diaper patrol!*" he shouted, letting out another burst of laughter that made his huge stomach shake. He turned and left the squad room, still laughing as he walked through the doorway.

Ted looked at his partners. "I wonder why they did pick us for this special assignment? We're all young, not too long out of the Academy and really still green about a lot of things," he said aloud.

Tony threw his hands up in the air, saying, "Holy, shit, Ted. Don't you know the answers to your own questions? We're young, intelligent, good looking, eager to learn, energetic and besides, we got small asses. That makes a harder target to hit. Now let's get downstairs and see what in the hell the captain wants."

The station house lobby was filled with the loud voices of people who were milling around. Most of the people were waiting to bail their friends and relatives out of jail. Ted's partners went into the captain's office, while Namsky went behind the large counter and retrieved a set of car keys for the unmarked squad car that they would be riding in.

A young girl of about fifteen years of age came running into the police station. She was both crying and screaming at the top of her voice. "Help me! Help me!"she cried. She leaned against a wall, covered her face with her hands and began to sob, hysterically.

Ted pulled up a chair and had her sit down. Everyone inside the captain's office came out to see what all the commotion was about.

"Now, young lady," said the desk sergeant, "take your time and tell us what's wrong."

The young girl stopped crying and wiped her eyes with her shirt sleeves. "It's my mother!" she whimpered. "She's gonna be hurt by a man!"

"What do you mean that she's going to be hurt? How?"asked the sergeant.

"I was at my girlfriend's house, a block away from here,"the young girl continued to speak, sobbing between phrases. "My mother called me there on the telephone. She said that someone was trying to get into our house! She told me to run over to this police station for help. My mother started to say something else, but the telephone went dead. Please help us before someone hurts my mother!"

"Where do you live, kid?"asked the sergeant, taking a pad of paper and a pencil out of his shirt pocket.

"214 Elliston Street - on the second floor!" she answered.

"Can't your mother use the back door to get away?" asked Ted.

"We have no back door,"the girl answered. "The old porch and stairway rotted. The carpenters tore them down and nailed the back door shut until they get the new porch and stairs built."

"What about the people living downstairs from you?" asked Ted. "Can't they help he until we get there?

The girl continued. "The first floor apartment is empty. No one has lived there for months!"

Ted walked over to Leon. "She only lives a block from here." he said. "Let's run over while the Sarge calls for some assist cars to cover us."

Ted was excited. He picked up his flashlight. The two officers ran out of the station as fast as their legs would carry them. In only a matter of minutes, the two officers were standing in front of 214 Elliston Street. The house lights were still on in the second floor apartment.

A good sign, thought Ted Namsky. The front door to the building was wide open. The officers waited a moment and just listened. The couldn't hear any noises, or voices.

"That window on the far side of the building looks like it could be their bedroom," said Leon. "I'm gonna try to shimmy up that drain pipe. I hope it holds me. Ted, go up the front way and cover them when they come out."

"Gotch-ya!" Ted took his gun out of the holster and darted up the front stairway.

Officer Bukowski pulled himself up the drain pipe as fast as his hands could pull him, under the strain. Ted stopped running and crept quietly up the remainder of the stairway leading to the second floor apartment.

Leon's fingers were raw and bleeding when he reached the window ledge. He used his fist to make a hole in the window screen. The window was partially open. He lifted it slowly and crawled into the apartment.

From the looks of the room, it belonged to the young girl. No one was in the bedroom. Leon stood still, and listened. He could hear heavy breathing. He crept slowly into the adjoining well-lighted room. It was the kitchen. It was empty also. The heavy breathing came from inside the living room.

From the kitchen, Leon could see another doorway on the right wall of the living room. He carefully worked his way next to the doorway and peeked into the room.

It was another bedroom. On a ruffled bed, lay an unconscious seminude woman. One man stood over her preparing himself to rape her while his partner rummaged through the dresser drawers.

Leon stood up and waited next to the doorway. He took his gun out of his holster and shouted loudly, "Police! Put your hands in the air and stand perfectly still!"

Both men lunged at Leon. He was hit in the midsection by one man while the other lifted him up into the air. Leon went flying backwards, tripping over the hassock, landing upside down on top of the couch.

The two suspects began to make their escape. One man jumped through the kitchen window, landing head first on the concrete sidewalk below the apartment. The other suspect ran through the front entrance doorway, smack dab - into Ted Namsky! Both Ted and the suspect tumbled down the stairs. The suspect got up and started to run away. Ted lay on the floor for a moment - stunned!

Leon opened the second floor living room window and shouted for the suspect to stop. The suspect froze, then quickly turned around and displayed a gun in his right hand. Officer Bukowski fired his revolver.

The suspect fell backwards, over a clump of hedges. His body lay limp. His face looked upwards towards the dark sky. Leon ran down the stairs and helped his partner to get up.

"You all right, Ted?" he asked.

"I'm O.K., Leon. Just had the wind knocked out of me for a moment. Where did that guy go?"

"He's out there in the grass,"answered Leon, pointing to the row of hedges.

Both officers walked over to where the suspect lay. His eyes stared blankly at the sky - seeing nothing. Blood trickled out of the corner of his mouth and left ear. The area, just above his left eyebrow, revealed a large hole. Blood oozed freely from the gaping hole. Ted bent over and felt the suspect's wrist, searching for a heart beat - but there was none.

"Better call for an ambulance,"said Leon, putting his revolver back into his holster.

"Don't need an ambulance for him," answered his partner. "We need the squadrol to transport him to the morgue. How's the woman doing?"

"I didn't really have the time to check, Ted, but from the looks of her, they worked her over real damn good. I'll go up and see how she is now. You stay down here with our two friends and wait for the squads to come. The guys should be here in a few minutes.

Leon turned and ran up the hallway stairs to the second floor apartment. Ted walked over to the second man, who had landed on his head. After looking at him for a moment, Ted knew there was no reason to feel his pulse. Half of his head was bashed in. Ted took his handkerchief out of his pants pocket and covered the suspect's head.

Two officers carried the injured woman down the flight of stairs on a stretcher.

"How is she?" asked the captain.

"I think she'll be all right,"answered one of the officers who was carrying the stretcher. "We'll know more when we get her to the hospital."

"You two did all right."said the captain, looking at Ted and his partner. "It's a good score for the new unit's first nights operation."

The unit's activities increased more and more with each passing day. In the first month alone, the number of district arrests doubled because of the efforts of the men in the new tactical unit. Being able to move around in plainclothes and unmarked cars, proved to be a valuable asset to the department. The men didn't rotate around the clock. Their basic working hours were from 8:00 p.m. until 4:00.a.m. These were the busiest hours in the district.

The tall, grey haired captain paced back and forth in front of his desk. Turning around, he sat on the edge of the desk and faced his men. Ted Namsky fumbled with his ball-point pen as he watched the captain.

"Men," spoke the captain, "you've done a great job in the short amount of time that we've had this unit. A problem has risen and we've been asked to take care of it. The Crowsdane Hotel has been having a big problem with robberies, burglaries and thefts. The hotel security force has been handling the problem, but it's gotten way out of hand. This morning, I had the owners of the Crowsdane Hotel in my office. They asked me to help them out. I told them that I would. I informed them about our new tactical team and told them that I would assign you four men to work with their people for the next two weeks."

Tony Seccoro raised his hand.

"Yes, Seccoro," said the captain.

"Captain," he paused, "I've always wanted to try my luck at being a bellhop. Can I wear one of those fancy suits and help all those pretty young ladies up to their bedrooms, just like they do it in the movies?"

The other officers,and the captain,laughed. Then the captain continued speaking. "Without you knowing it, Seccoro, you hit it right on the head. That's just what I had in mind for you. All four of you will be placed into a working position that will enable you to watch people, gather information and move around the hotel without being picked out as being police officers. I read over your personnel folders and discussed them with the owners of the hotel. They totally agree with the selections that I have made for you all."

"Officer Seccoro,you'll be assigned to work as a bellhop. Officer Bukowski, you've had some experience mixing drinks, so you'll work as a bartender assigned to the lounge area. Officer Barner, you'll work in the maintenance section of the building as a general handyman. Officer Namsky, you're to work out of the kitchen as a waiter, handling room service. All of you will report to a Mister Jamison, who is in charge of the hotel security force. He's the only one, besides the owners of the hotel, who will know who you fellows really are. Be careful! Be alert! Do a good job. See you all back here in two weeks."

The four officers left the captain's office and went up to the locker room.

"We'll drive over to the hotel in my car," Tony Seccoro offered. "No sense in us taking four cars over there."

"Great!" replied Ted, "and while you're at it, will you carry my attaché case down to the car? You might as well get some experience as a bellhop. Besides, I might even give you a good tip."

"Tip your ass, Namsky!" snapped Tony Seccoro.

The four officers were laughing as they walked down the stairway and out into the street.

CHAPTER XIX

The first week in their new undercover positions went along on a regular, routine schedule. Tony seccoro's undercover position was changed at the last minute. He was registered as a hotel guest instead of working as a bellhop.

On Tuesday, of the second week, all hell broke loose. The officers had blown their undercover identities. It all started about 8:30 p.m. that night. The large, leather covered bar in the lounge was three-quarter filled with drinking customers. Leon Bukowski had just finished mixing two Bacardis for two young women sitting at the far end of the bar.

As one of the girls opened her purse to pay the bar bill, Officer Bukowski spotted a lock pulling device at the bottom of her purse. Walking past them, He had caught some of their conversation. From what he had heard, Leon surmised that they were probably a couple of call girls, as well as possible burglars.

The taller of the two girls ordered two more Bacardis. Leon mixed the drinks and placed them in front of the girls. He removed the empty glasses and placed them into a sink.

"Are you two staying at this hotel?" he asked, trying to strike up a conversation.

The shorter of the two girls picked up her glass, sipped the cold fluid casually, then said, "We're just visiting a friend who's staying here."

"Are you both local girls or are you from out of town?" Leon continued his questioning. "I'm from out of town myself. I just blew in from Tucson last week. I've only been a bartender here for about a week now. Sure would like to meet someone from this town. I don't know anyone, personally.

The young woman finished the rest of her drink before responding to Leon. "Can I ask you a question?"

"Sure, " Leon replied, very curious.

"How much do you make a week as a bartender?"

"About two hundred bucks - clear." he replied, a puzzled look on his face. "Why?

"Honey!" she continued, "when you make a *'Grand'* a week clear, *then* you and I will get together, but not until then. So why don't you just go and polish your fifty-cent beer glasses - asshole!"

Leon had a very funny feeling about these two girls. He was sure that he had them pegged right. One of the hotel bellhops passed through the lounge area, on his way to the men's washroom. Leon got an idea.

"Hey, Tommy!" he shouted. "Come over here for a minute. I want to ask you for a favor."

The bellhop came over to the bar, standing not more than two feet away from the two women.

"What can I do for you?" asked the bellhop.

Leon leaned over the bar, giving the appearance that he didn't want anyone to hear him. And yet, he spoke loudly enough for the two women to hear. "Tommy," he said, when he was sure that he had attracted their attention, "there was a guy from Room 1214 in the lounge earlier in the evening. He asked me if I knew where he could get some female companions for tonight. He said he was a salesman from Dallas, Texas. Man, was he flashing a wad of dough! This guy tells me that if I could come up with a couple of good looking dolls, there'd be a 'C' note in it for me. Hell, I'm new in this town. I don't know of any gals who'd be interested. Can you help me out? I'll split the 'C' note with you if you can come up with the broads."

The bellhop shrugged his shoulders and said, "Hell, I don't know of anyone that I could get on the spur of the moment. Let me ask around and I'll get back to you in a little while. O.K.?"

"Great. Give it your best shot!" Leon replied as he started drying another glass. "See you later, Tommy," he said as the bellhop went on his way.

The two women quickly finished their drinks and left the lounge. Leon knew where they were going. He watched one of the women write down the room number that he had given to the bellhop. Officer Bukowski picked up the house phone and dialed Room 1214. The line was busy.

Damn! he thought. Who is he talking to now? Leon re-dialed the number and waited. The line was still busy. "Shit!" Leon mumbled as he dialed another telephone number and waited.

"Maintenance room," said the voice at the other end of the line. Leon didn't recognize the voice.

"Is there a man available to fix a leak in the sink in the lounge?" he asked.

"We have a man," replied the voice, "but he's out on another job right now. He should be back in about fifteen minutes. I'll send Tim up to see you as soon as he gets back."

"Good!" Leon replied, then hung up. He looked at his wrist watch. Fifteen minutes should be enough time for those two to carry out their plans, thought Leon. He dialed Room 1214 again. The line was still busy. He dialed the kitchen. That line was busy, too.

Tony knows what to do, Leon tried to convince himself. He knows what plan to use when he comes in contact with a suspect. When everything was set, Tony was to call room service and order some food. Then he was to call the bar for some drinks and let the maintenance room to report a problem with his toilet. This would get everyone up to his room to help him make the arrest.

The patrons at the bar became bothersome for more drinks. Leon didn't want to blow his cover. He quickly obliged them and made the drinks that they wanted.

Tony Seccoro lay on his bed, his hands tucked behind his head, watching a night baseball game on television. There was a knock at the door.

"Who is it?" he shouted. Another knock. Still no answer. "Shit!" Tony grunted as he rolled off the bed and turned down the TV. He walked over to the door and opened it.

The two young women from the bar stood in the hallway, each one displaying a sweet, innocent smile.

"What can I do for you two beautiful young ladies?" Tony asked, clearing his throat as he spoke.

"It's not what you can do for us, baby, " spoke the taller woman. "The question is, what can *we* do for *you*?"

Tony hesitated a moment, then continued to play along with the two women. "It all depends on who sent you to see me, " he laughed as he spoke.

"Let's quit playing games,"interrupted the shorter woman."The bartender down in the lounge called our room and told us to come to this room if we wanted to see some real action. I don't like standing in hallways." The woman pulled down the front of her dress until the nipple of her left breast was visible. "If it's sex that you want, then we're here for it. Now, do you invite us in or do we leave?"

"Hey! You're a lively one!"said Officer Seccoro, smiling as he stepped aside to let the two women enter his room. "That bartender really came through with some real... humdingers. If you girls are as good as you both look, I'm gonna drop that bartender an extra bonus!"

The two women walked into the room, giving it a quick survey, Tony dropped down into a lounge chair and lit up a cigarette. The women made themselves comfortable on the soft, plush velvet sofa.

"My name's Tony, " he said.

"I'm Gera and my friend's name is Luise." said the taller of the two. "Now, do you want us both at once, or one at a time, and do you want straight sex or oral?"

"Say," he laughed, striking out his cigarette in the ashtray, "you girls sure don't beat around the bush in this here city. I thought we'd get acquainted first before we got down to business. You know - a little food - a little booze - some goofing around. Stuff like that!"

"Listen! This is a business for us, mister. Time is money,"said the shorter woman. "If you wanted someone to wine and dine, you should have checked the lonely heart ads in the newspaper." She started to get up from the sofa.

"O.K.! O.K.! Just hold it!" Tony shouted. "If you want to talk shop, what's the going price?" he asked.

"$250.00 a girl." answered the taller woman, kicking off her shoes.

"Wheeeeeeeee!" whistled Tony, standing up. "That's a little high, isn't it?"

"Look, pal," interrupted the shorter woman, "if you want gutter *'shit'* for five and ten bucks, then go out and pick some ass off the street corner, and maybe you'll get a good case of the clap along with it. If you want the first class merchandise, that's us! And baby, you're going to have to pay plenty for it."

"O.K.! O.K.!" said Tony, laughing. "You're both hired. I want both of you. You've just convinced me. Do you want your money before or after?" he asked.

"You can pay now, and then play." replied the taller woman, showing Tony her best seductive smile.

Reaching down into his pants pocket, Officer Seccoro took out a large roll of marked bills and counted off $250.00 for each woman. He put the remainder of the money back into his pocket. The two women carefully watched every move that Tony made.

"How would it be if I called room service for some drinks and food? Screwing always makes me hungry." He picked up the phone.

"For Christ sake, order that Goddamn food!" said the angered shorter woman as she kicked off her shoes and removed her nylon stockings.

Tony dialed the number for the lounge and waited. Finally, after several rings, someone picked up the telephone. "Lounge bar." replied the voice. Tony didn't recognize the voice.

"Hey, how come it took you so damn long to answer the phone?" he snapped angrily.

"Hey, pal,' answered the voice, "I'm the only bartender here right now. If you want to place an order, fine. If you don't, I haven't got time to bullshit with you over the phone!"

"This is Room 1214. Send up a bottle of Scotch, some ice, glasses and a couple of bottles of club soda," said Tony, hoping that Leon would hurry and get back to the bar and get the message. "And bartender," he continued, "hurry it up."

"Yes, sir!" the voice responded sarcastically. Then the phone went dead.

Tony quickly dialed the kitchen. All he could get was a busy signal. I'll just have to stall the girls, he thought, until Leon gets the message and comes up. If he doesn't get here soon, I'll have to make the bust myself.

The taller woman got up from the sofa, walked over to Officer Seccoro, took the phone out of his hand and placed it down on its cradle. She placed both of her arms around his neck, pressed her body as close to his as she could, then kissed him softly on his lips as she grasped his penis with her right hand.

"Now," she said, "we're ready. Why don't you go into the bedroom and get ready for a wild experience while we finish undressing out here?"

"Oh boy!" exclaimed Tony, feigning great excitement. "I'll take you on one at a time!"

The shorter woman began removing her dress. Tony watched her as he walked backwards into the bedroom. He had his back to the doorway as he slowly began to undress. He didn't see the two women quietly sneak into the bedroom. Bending over to untie his shoelace, a great moving force hit him on his backside, sending him flying face down onto the carpeted floor.

Stunned for a second, Tony then realized what had just happened as he felt the pressure of a sharp pointed object being placed at the base of his skull.

"Don't make a single move, sweetheart!" said a woman's voice. "I've got an ice pick at the base of your neck. One false move and it's 'bye-bye' for you. Understand?"

"Yes," Tony grunted as the woman sat down on his back.

"Good, sweetheart, I'm glad we understand each other." She continued. "Now slowly place your hands behind you - one at a time."

Tony followed her instructions without hesitation.

"That's a good boy," she remarked, laughing. She bound his hands together with a piece of lamp cord that the other woman had gotten for her. He heard the sound of material being torn. Tony almost choked when the woman stuffed some of the bed sheet into his mouth. She used the rest of the bedsheet to wrap around his mouth.

"Now get up slowly," she ordered.

Tony felt a great relief as she got off him. With great difficulty, he managed to stand up. It was the shorter of the two women who was giving the orders and holding the ice pick. She clutched her fist tightly and hit him in the stomach with all the power that she possessed in her arm. Tony fell backwards onto the bed, groaning with unbearable pain.

"Good boy," said the tall woman as she removed his pants. After emptying the contents of his pockets onto the middle of the bedroom floor, she picked up the large roll of bills and counted it. "Twelve hundred bucks. Not bad for fifteen minute's work."

"Yeah," agreed the other woman, removing the rest of Tony's clothes. "And the poor dumb-fuck didn't even get his jollies off. Gee, that's too bad."

They tied Tony's legs together with another piece of lamp cord. Both women stood at the foot of the bed and carefully studied Tony's nude body.

"You know," said the taller of the two women, "he's hung pretty good. I'm getting a little horny. It's a shame that we have to go." They both laughed as they threw all of Tony's clothes out of the hotel window. The clothes landed on the roof top of a shorter building below.

Leon Bukowski came back to the bar when the other bartender was placing the Scotch, club soda, ice and glasses onto a cart.

"Everything come out all right?" asked the bartender as he wheeled the cart out from behind the bar.

Leon just smiled. "I just made it to the *John* in time. Next time, I won't wait so long. Where are you going with the cart?" he asked.

"Room 1214," the bartender answered.

"*Room 1214!*" Leon shouted. "What time did you get the call?"

"I don't know exactly - maybe fifteen minutes ago while you were relieving yourself," answered the bewildered bartender, not knowing why Officer Bukowski was so agitated.

Listen," said Leon, "let me take this order up to that room."

"No," said the bartender, reluctantly. "You stay here and take care of the cash customers. If I get a big tip, I'll split it with you - don't worry!"

Officer Bukowski could see that he wasn't going to get anywhere by arguing with the other bartender. He reached into his pants pocket and showed the bartender his police badge. "This is official business! The man in 1214 is an undercover police officer, too. That's why I'm taking up this cart!"

"A cop!" exclaimed the surprised bartender. "Well I'll be damned. You guys are moonlighting everywhere these days."

Leon dialed the kitchen and asked for Ted Namsky. He was delivering a room service food order. Leon finally reached Tim Barner in the maintenance room.

"Tim, this is Leon," he said. "We got a couple of live ones up in Room 1214. Meet me up there - on the double!" Leon pressed the dial tone button and re-dialed Room 1214. The line kept buzzing. No one answered.

Shit! he thought, as he hung up the receiver and pushed the cart towards the service elevator.

Leon knocked on the door of Room 1214 and waited. No one answered. He turned the doorknob, pushed open the door and walked into the room. "Tony!" he shouted. "Tony, are you all right?"

A muffled groan came from the direction of the bedroom. Leon rushed into the bedroom, with his gun drawn and burst out in laughter at the scene that he saw before him. There on the bed before him, lay Tony Seccoro, tied up and stark naked. Tony rolled back and forth, furiously trying to free himself.

"Take it easy, pal," said Leon, wiping the tears from his eyes. "I'll have you free in just a moment." He removed the gag from around Tony's mouth.

"You big asshole!" Tony shouted angrily. "Hurry up and get these cords off my hands and feet.

"O.K. Just take it easy." said Leon, trying to calm down his partner. "Hey, Tony, I didn't know you had a beauty mark just above your belly button."

"Screw you, Leon," Tony mumbled after he was untied. He got up off the bed. Removing the bedsheet, he wrapped it around himself.

Tim Barner entered the bedroom. Upon seeing Tony wrapped in the bedsheet, he shouted, "Hail - Caesar!"

"O.K.!" Leon interrupted, now becoming serious. "Who tied you up, Tony? Was it two dames?"

"Yeah, the same two that you sent up here."

"I didn't send them up here." said Leon. "I was talking with a bellhop and the women overheard our conversation. I figured that they were a couple of hookers, but I couldn't get close to them. I laid out a little bait by insinuating that you were a loaded salesman looking to buy some hot snatch for the night. They took it from there. Say, where in the hell are your clothes?"

"They threw them out the damn window just before they left," Tony answered, disgusted..

"You stay here, Tony. Tim and I will look for those two women in the hotel."

"Like hell you will!" Tony angrily shouted. "I'm not staying here. I'm going with you to find those two lousy bitches!"

The three officers searched the entire twelfth floor - Leon, Tim and Tony Seccoro, still wrapped in his bedsheet. Hotel guests saw them walking around and telephoned the hotel security office, stating that there were strange looking men roaming around the halls.

When the three officers reached the tenth floor, they spotted the two women forcing their way into one of the hotel rooms.

"There they are!" yelled Tony Seccoro.

Upon seeing the three officers, one women dropped the lock pulling device and both of them ran down the long hallway.

As the two women ran past the elevator doors, they opened. Officers Barner and Bukowski ran past the elevator, just before Ted Namsky stepped off, pushing a cart loaded with food. Officer Seccoro ran smack dab into the cart. Food flew in every direction. The bedsheet was pulled off Tony during the collision with the cart. His body was covered with lettuce, salad dressing, steak sauce and catsup! He lay stunned on the floor.

Two elderly women came out of their hotel room just after the collision with the cart. Upon seeing Tony's naked body on the floor, covered with food and sauces, they both screamed and fainted.

The two female suspects were about to make their escape down the exit stairway, when they were grabbed by Leon and Tim. Both women deliberately tore open the fronts of their dresses, exposing their bare breasts. "Robbery! Rape! Muggers! Someone help us!" the two women screamed.

The hotel was swarming with security police who eventually apprehended the two women - and the four police officers. In the security office, Leon Bukowski tried desperately to convince the hotel security officers that they were really undercover policemen.

In the struggle with the two women, Leon had lost his wallet, with all of his identification. Officers Namsky and Barner had forgotten their stars and I.D. cards in their lockers, back at the police station.

The hotel security officer tried for several hours to reach either the Chief of Security or one of the hotel owners to verify Leon Bukowski's undercover story. He finally succeeded in locating one of the hotel owners. Their stories were verified. The two women were searched by two police women who had been brought to the hotel. They found all of the marked money tucked in one of the suspect's panties. Both women were taken to the district station to be booked and processed.

CHAPTER XX

Problems of the EL trains had developed to overwhelming proportions. Pickpocketing, robberies, purse snatchings, rapes and homicides had all increased considerably. The Brass in the *Ivory Towers* decided to have the new tactical teams concentrate all their efforts on the EL trains.

Officers Namsky, Barner, Bukowski and Seccoro were selected to dress as women - acting as decoys on the trains. In the first two weeks of operation, forty-two felons were apprehended and booked for court.

Ted Namsky looked at his wrist watch. 10:30 p.m. The train wheels screeched and clattered as they rapidly moved along the metal tracks. Ted stared at the reflection in the darkened window next to him.

Ugh! he thought. I sure make an ugly looking broad. He straightened his blond wig. How in the hell do women always manage to keep track of their damn purse? he mumbled as he fumbled with it clumsily on his lap. It was heavy because of the service revolver inside.

It felt unusually warm inside the EL car. Ted opened his window to let in some fresh air.

Only half an hour more, he thought, then I'll be able to get out of this *Drag* outfit and back into men's clothes.

The train stopped at the Fulton Street Station to take on, and let passengers off. Officer Namsky took special notice of a tall, lanky man dressed in a sports jacket, white shirt, tie and straw hat. The man entered the EL car, walked to the opposite end, then sat down, facing Officer Namsky. Ted quickly looked around. Including himself, there were two other passengers besides the lanky man.

The man watched Ted's movements for several minutes. Realizing that he was being stared at, Ted put on a little act. He removed a silver compact from his purse, pretending to be putting on some fresh make-up. The man continued to watch him. Ted put away his compact.

Looking at the man, Ted revealed a shy, sly smile. The man returned the smile. Ted knew that he was going to make another bust before the night was over. The man got up from his seat, walked over to Officer Namsky and sat down next to him.

"Hi!" whispered the man. "My name's Charley. What's yours?"

"Cindy," Ted answered, coughing slightly, trying to disguise his voice.

"Say, Cindy, I'm new in town. Do you know where I can get some good female action?"

Ted played the game. "Sure, Charley, I'll get you all of the action you can handle."

"What's the charge going to be, honey?"

"When I'm through," Ted continued, "you can pay me what ever you think I'm worth."

"Great!" exclaimed Charley, grabbing Officer Namsky's right wrist.

Ted quickly pulled his hand away from his lap, sending his purse sailing through the open window. "Oh, no!" he groaned.

"That's all right," said Charley as he quickly slapped a set of handcuffs onto Ted's wrists. He produced a badge. "The name's Murphy! Officer Murphy to you, of downtown Vice. You're under arrest, honey, for solicitation!"

"Wait. Listen!" Ted pleaded, quickly removing his wig. "I'm a cop, too. I'm working undercover on this EL detail, too."

"Well I'll be damned," laughed Officer Murphy. "You're not even a real dame. Just a guy, and probably a rapist, too! And, claiming to be a cop to boot. They'll never believe me when I tell them this story at home. Now just take it easy, fella. We'll be at the police station in no time at all."

"No - wait - listen!" Ted pleaded. "I really am a police officer."

"Sure - sure - sure!" laughed Officer Murphy. "Then show me your badge if you're a cop."

Officer Namsky started to reach for his pants pocket, then remembered that he had his identification as well as his gun in the purse - and it had gone sailing out the window!

"Can't produce any proof, huh?" said Officer Murphy, now starting to get angry. "I thought so. Now just take it easy or you'll get your ass broken if you give me any more trouble! Hear me!"

The train stopped at the downtown police headquarters station. Officer Namsky was quickly ushered off the train.

"Wait a minute." Ted started to plead again. "Look, I really am a cop. If you book me and put me through the regular paper work, we'll both be the laughing stock of our units. All I'm asking is that you call my sergeant at the number I give you."

"Save the conversation, pal." interrupted Officer Murphy. "As far as your call goes, you'd better use it to call your lawyer."

Ted was escorted up to the Men's Central Detention Lockup, continually protesting that he was a police officer. He was searched, fingerprinted and photographed.

A half-hour had passed when the lockup keeper brought back the results from the Identification Section.

"Hey! Murphy!" yelled the lockup keeper.

"Yeah. What is it?" Murphy answered as he finished taking a drink at the water fountain.

"Look at this." The lockup keeper handed the results of the fingerprint check to Officer Murphy. He read the report. "I'll be Goddamned! He really is a cop. Bring him out of the cell."

Two minutes later the lockup keeper brought Ted up to the front office. Officer Murphy held out his hand. "Glad to meet you, Officer Namsky. Sorry we had to do it this way, but you understand - it's regulations."

"I told you that I was a cop!" Ted snapped angrily.

"But you couldn't produce any kind of identification." said Officer Murphy.

"I had my identification in that damn purse that went flying out that train window."

"Oh, by the way, Officer Namsky," said Officer Murphy, "I just checked with Communications and they informed me that the purse was recovered by a beat officer. He saw the purse fall from the train window. I'll get a pool car and we'll drive over to the 13th District Station and pick it up. Then, if you'd like, I'll drive you back to your unit so you can change clothes."

"That's fine with me," Ted answered, placing his wig back on top of his head. He pressed the elevator button and waited.

The lockup keeper, sitting behind his desk, jokingly remarked, "Officer Namsky, don't feel bad about how things worked out. You still make a pretty nice looking dame!"

The elevator doors opened. Officers Namsky and Murphy entered the elevator. Just before the elevator doors closed, Ted shouted, *Balls!* at the lockup keeper.

CHAPTER XXI

March had arrived very quickly. It was only three months before Ted and Tracy's wedding day.

Ted was working the late afternoon watch. Tracy managed to get the same working hours as Ted, at the hospital. She looked at her wrist watch. 2:30 p.m. She gave her car horn two quick hits. Two minutes later, Ted came running out the front door of his rooming house. He got into her car and gave her a quick kiss on the cheek.

"Sorry I'm late, honey," he said as he straightened his tie. "I had some shopping to do this afternoon and got home later than I had planned."

"Tracy smiled, turning on the ignition switch. The engine groaned and sputtered a few times, then went silent. "It'll be fine in a minute," she said. "It's the stupid carburetor again. Sometimes it floods." She turned on the ignition switch again. The car finally started.

"After we're married," he said, "we're going to get you a new car. I don't think this one will last too much longer."

"Yes, dear," she answered, gently blowing him a kiss.

They stopped in front of the district station some twenty minutes later.

"Pick you up about 12:30," she said as he got out of the car.

"Right! See you tonight after the shift ends." He leaned forward into the car, gave her a quick kiss and ran into the station.

The hospital was busy throughout the entire day. Before Tracy had realized, it was 11:30 p.m. The relief nurse came over to Tracy's desk. "Here I am, Tracy," she said.

"Hi, Jean. Glad you got here a few minutes early."

"You going to pick up Ted tonight?" asked the relief nurse.

"Yes, but I have to stop at the gas station for some gas and cigarettes before I pick him up."

"Be careful," shouted the relief nurse as Tracy started to leave the hospital. Tracy turned slightly, smiled, gave a quick wave, then ran out to the parking lot.

Tracy unlocked the car door and got in. She switched on the ignition switch. Nothing happened. She waited a moment, then tried it again. This time the car started. It ran for a short time, then there was a loud noise from the engine, and it quit running.

Tracy got out of the car and raised the hood. A puff of smoke rose quickly towards the sky. "Oh dear!" she remarked as she shut the hood and ran back into the hospital.

"Back already?" asked the relief nurse.

"I think my car finally had a nervous breakdown," said Tracy, laughing. She picked up the telephone and dialed the number for Ted's station.

"Twelfth District," answered the desk officer.

"Is Officer Namsky in the station yet?" she asked.

"No, miss," the officer answered. "He got a call from the dispatcher and had to go back on the street for awhile."

"Thank you," she replied, then hung up the telephone.

"Did you reach Ted?" asked the relief nurse.

"No," Tracy answered, a little worried.

"What are you going to do, Tracy?" asked the relief nurse. "Stay here and wait for him?"

"No, I think I'll walk down to the bus stop and take a bus over to the station and wait for him over there."

"Tracy, it's a two block walk to the bus stop. The busses only run every half hour at this time of night. It's dangerous for a young girl to be walking out on those streets by herself this late. Let me call a guard or an intern to walk with you to the bus stop. He'll stay with you until a bus comes." said the relief nurse, very concerned.

"Nonsense," Tracy laughed. "I'll be all right. There's plenty of traffic moving around on the street. Don't worry so much. It'll give you a lot of wrinkles and gray hair."

Tracy Tate left the hospital before the relief nurse could say another word. She walked quickly, reaching the bus stop in a matter of minutes. Glancing at her watch, she saw that it was ten minutes past twelve. Tracy strained her eyes, trying to see if a bus was coming in the far off distance. No bus was in sight. She waited.

A short while later, a white Lincoln sedan, occupied by two males, pulled up in front of her and stopped.

"Hey, honey, going our way?" asked the man sitting in the passenger seat. "Come on, sweetstuff, wiggle your pretty little ass and get into the car!"

At first, Tracy ignored the remarks, but then she felt frightened. She realized that she was in some kind of danger. The man continued to talk as he brought a pint bottle of whiskey up to his lips and took a long swallow. He held out the bottle towards Tracy.

"Come on, baby, don't play hard to get. Make it easy on yourself. You know, foxy lady, I'm gonna get you in the long run, anyway. Come on, get in the car and have a drink of booze with us. We'll go and park somewhere and I'll show you how good of a man I am!"

Tracy couldn't speak. She was terrified! Turning quickly, she started to run away. The man sprinted out of the car and ran after her. He caught up with her within half a block. His partner drove the car up next to them and got out to help his friend..

Tracy was grabbed around her waist and dragged towards the car. She screamed as loud as she could. The first man drew back his fist and punched her in the face. Blood squirted from both of her nostrils, causing her to gag and choke. She managed to clear her throat and let out another scream.

"Shut up, bitch!" screamed the man, raising his fist, then striking her in the face again.

"Grab her legs, Pete!" ordered the second man.

Tracy began kicking like a scared mule, making it impossible for the man to grab hold of her legs. She screamed again. And again, the man called Pete punched her in the face. Both her eyes were badly swollen. It was hard for Tracy to see. Blood flowed freely from her nose and mouth, but she still continued to scream. Someone had heard her cries for help and called the police. The loud wail of screaming sirens in the far off distance made the two men stop for a moment and listen.

"All right, bitch, stay here if you like," screamed Pete as he knocked Tracy to the ground. "But, I'm gonna fix you up real good so that you'll always remember us."

Pete quickly looked around the area, searching for something on the ground. Seeing a piece of broken curb concrete laying in the dirt, he grabbed it and raised it above his head.

"This will teach you to give us a rough time - *bitch*!" he muttered crazily.

"No! Please don't!" pleaded Tracy, in a whimpering voice. "Please don't hurt me anymore!"

Pete drove the rock down into her forehead - once - twice - then one more time for good measure.

"Come on, man. Let's go! The cops are almost here!" shouted Pete's partner from inside the car. He raced the car engine wildly. Pete got off Tracy, removed the whiskey bottle from his pocket, smashed it on the sidewalk and jabbed the jagged edge of the glass into the side of Tracy's neck, then ran to the car. The two men sped off, leaving a trail of screeching, smoking tire marks.

Sergeant Conley was waiting for Officer Namsky when he came into the police station.

"Want to see me about something special, Sarge?" asked Ted, leisurely strolling up to the sergeant's desk.

"Yes, Ted,"Sergeant Conley replied sadly. He couldn't look Ted straight in the eyes when he had to break the bad news to him. "You'd better get over to Christian Hospital right away, Ted!"

"What's up, Sarge?"

"It's your girlfriend, Ted. She's had a bad accident. She's in pretty bad shape."

"What's happened to her, Sarge? How is she?" Ted pleaded for some kind of an answer.

"Don't waste precious time here asking questions, Ted. Get right over there as fast as you can. I don't know how much time she has left," the sergeant said sadly.

"Come on, let's go!" shouted Tony Seccoro. "I'll drive us to the hospital!"

Ted rushed into the waiting room. He ran over to Tracy's friend, the relief nurse.

"Jean. Where's Tracy?" he asked, afraid to hear what she had to say. "How is she?"

The relief nurse, her eyes red and swollen from crying, slowly looked up at Ted. "She's upstairs in surgery, Ted," she answered, half talking and half crying, "She's in real bad shape, Ted!" she whimpered.

"What - what happened to her?" he asked.

"Her car wouldn't start. We tried to call you at the station, but you were out on a call. She decided to take a bus to the police station and wait for you there. As far as anyone can figure, someone tried to drag her into a car. She put up one hell of a good fight! She was beaten up. She was stabbed in the neck with a piece of glass and her skull was crushed. Honest-to-God, Ted, I tried to talk her out of going. I told her to wait here for you. I tried to stop her, Ted, I tried to stop her!" sobbed the relief nurse.

Ted took the elevator up to the floor where the surgical waiting room was located. Tony went with him.

Ted paced the floor, back and forth, smoking cigarette after cigarette, while drinking cup after cup of coffee. He spoke to no one while he was waiting.

Concluding four hours of torturous waiting, the doctor finally came to the waiting room. His surgical smock was covered with blood and pieces of human flesh. A perspiration stain soiled the front of his cap. All Ted could say was, "Doc?"

"I'm very sorry, Officer Namsky. Tracy didn't make it. She put up a hell of a fight to stay alive, but the odds were against her. I'm sorry." said the doctor, sadly.

Ted dropped the cup of coffee that he was holding and sat down on the leather couch. He bent over, covering his face with both of his hands, and wept: he was broken hearted.

"I'll take care of him, Doc," said Tony Seccoro, picking up the coffee cup. He sat down next to his partner, placing his hand on his shoulder. "I'm real sorry, Ted," he whispered softly, finding it hard to speak to his friend, "I'm truly sorry," Tony whispered again.

It was a very hot summer in more ways then one. A civil rights leader was killed and riots broke out in all parts of the city. Total unrest broke out everywhere.

Ted tried desperately to catch the killers of Tracy. He questioned the people in the houses that lived in the area of the attack. Other that hearing Tracy's screams and seeing a car pull away from the scene, the old woman who called the police that night couldn't furnish Ted with any other information.

Ted checked arrest reports of persons in the area that night - traffic citations of cars in the area - any and all reports that had anything to do with the area of the attack. He came up with - nothing. Tracy's attackers had gotten away clean - without even a trace to their identities. Even the latent fingerprints that were found on the broken bottle turned out to be useless smudges.

CHAPTER XXII

It took Ted several months after Tracy's funeral, before he could get partial composure. He was truly a changed man! It showed in every task that he performed. He now took too many unnecessary chances. To the men he worked with, it seemed as if he didn't care about anything, anymore. He never spoke of Tracy again.

It was early August. The weather was hot. Over 100 degrees for ten days. A police squad car had run over a young boy and killed him. The officer driving the car was answering a call for *Help*. The four year old child had darted out from between two parked cars. The officer didn't see the child, until it was too late.

The people in the neighborhood went wild with anger over the young child's death. Police vehicles were constantly being bombarded with rocks and bottles. Snipers fired at the police - stores were looted. Molotov cocktails were dropped on passing cars from the overpasses onto the expressways. Havoc and destruction broke out all over the city once more. Police officers were put on twelve and eighteen hour working shifts. All days off were canceled. The Mayor had declared the city *"To be in a State of Emergency!"*

Ted reported for duty at 6:30 p.m., dressed in full uniform, wearing his riot helmet. He entered the squad room. Most of the men from his shift were already there. Tim Barner, Leon Bukowski and Tony Seccoro sat on a bench at the far end of the room. Ted waved, but didn't feel like talking, so he just sat down at the first available space that he came across.

A few minutes passed. The captain entered the squad room. "Just remain seated!" he said as he stepped up to the podium. "Men," he began, "I don't have to explain the situation to you. You all know what's happening out on those streets. From now on, I want four-man squad cars patrolling the streets. I want all of you to be alert. Give special attention to the liquor stores and drugstores. For any type of infraction of the laws, I want suspects brought in and booked. Officers Namsky, Seccoro, Barner and Bukowski, you men will ride together in beat car-1242. There are ten liquor stores and four drugstores on your assigned beat. Keep a sharp eye on all of them."

The captain assigned the rest of the men to their patrol beats, then dismissed them for patrol duty.

"Car, 1242!" paged the dispatcher's voice from the speaker.

"1242," Tony answered.

"1242, investigate strange noises coming from the alleyway at Clinton and Justine Streets."

"We're on our way, squad." Tony replied.

"Ten-four - 1242."

Ted pressed the gas pedal to the floor. Within three minutes they were entering the alleyway on Justine Street. The blue and white slowed down and cruised along - slowly.

"Watch out, Ted! There's a cable strung between those two telephone poles!" Tony Seccoro shouted, but it was too late. The squad car had already passed over the cable and snapped it. The metal wire wrapped itself around the drive shaft like a boa constrictor choking its' prey.

Ted stopped the car for a moment, then proceeded to move on. Each foot that he advanced made the cable wire wind itself tighter and tighter around the drive shaft, until the universal joint on the drive shaft snapped. The squad car was immobile! Leon spotted a figure lurking in the shadows, a short distance from them. "Hey! Something's moving next to that garage - over there!" he shouted. A man's figure stepped out of the shadows into the middle of the alley. The dark figure held a long object in his hands.

"Hit the floor!" Ted shouted. "He's got a shotgun in his hands!"

The figure pointed the weapon towards the squad car's windshield and fired. The windshield and rear window shattered into thousands of tiny pieces of glass. Lead pellets ricocheted inside the squad car, hitting everyone, but not hard enough to do any real injury to them.

Ted removed his revolver from his holster, opened the car door slowly, then hit the ground on his stomach. Rolling over, he hid behind a metal garbage can. By the time he could aim his revolver, the dark figure was gone.

"Is everyone O.K.?" Ted shouted.

"Yeah, Ted," replied Tony.

"Tony," Ted continued, "turn on the spotlight and scan the entire alley!"

Tony turned on the beam of light and slowly shined it from one side of the alley to the other. Nothing could be seen - moving or hiding.

"I guess it's all right now," said Officer Namsky. He picked himself up from the dirty concrete. "Looks like there was only one of them. He's probably the one who made the phone call and then waited for us."

Officer Seccoro picked up the microphone from the squad car floor and made a call for help. Within minutes, six squad cars were on the scene. A search was made, but no suspect could be found.

A city tow truck removed the disabled squad car from the alley. The four officers were driven back to the station and issued another car for patrol duty.

"What time is it, Leon?" Tim asked, shaking his wrist. "My watch stopped."

"A quarter past eight," Leon answered.

"Anyone want to get a bite to eat?" asked Tony. "My stomach's kicking up a storm." They all agreed to stop for something to eat.

The *Stop And Fill It* Restaurant had just been open for two weeks. It was small, but the food was good and the prices were right.

They had finished their meals and gotten into their squad car. An *All Out Emergency* call came from the Communications dispatcher. "Attention all cars! The looting has started again. All cars proceed to your assigned patrol beats!"

Ted started the squad car and sped off, heading for the biggest drugstore on their beat. People were running crazily through the street, smashing car windows, store windows and street lights. Ted had guessed right. When they had reached the T&M Drugstore, there was already a crowd gathering around the front door. Directly across the street at the Royton Drugstore, the same situation was occurring.

"Tim and Leon! Guard the Royton Drugstore!" shouted Ted. "Tony and I will guard T&M."

They all put on their riot helmets and exited the squad car. Ted unlocked the trunk. Officers Bukowski and Barner removed two shotguns and ran across the street to the Royton Drugstore. Tony guarded the front entrance of T&M, while Ted drove the squad car around to the back door. Since both drugstores were located on corners it was easy for Officer Namsky to view the stores across the street, as well as the back door of the drugstore.

It had happened again. This was going to be another night of hell! People ran through the streets shouting and cursing. A crowd was beginning to gather across the street from Officer Namsky, in front of a Five And Dime novelty store. Ted studied the crowd carefully, then realized what was actually coming down.

Some older men in the crowd were encouraging younger people and children to break the store windows, go inside and get merchandise for them. A second group of men waited and carefully watched all of Ted's movements. Suddenly, the sound of a loud crash filled the night air. A large plate glass window in the front of the Five And Dime ruptured, spilling large hunks of glass everywhere. The crowd cheered in approval.

The children began climbing into the novelty store through the large gapping hole in the glass.

My God, thought Ted. If that glass falls while those kids are crawling under it, they'll be killed! Ted ran over to the curb.

A man across the street yelled, "Here comes the cop!" Most of the crowd moved away from the Five And Dime, except for a small group of men who were watching Ted Namsky. They started across the street. Ted knew what they were after. He stepped back from the curb, keeping an eye on the movement of the crowd. He finally reached the rear door of the drugstore.

The crowd across the street moved forward again towards the novelty store. More children crawled into the store through the large hole in the window. Items of clothing, toys, small T.V.'s and various other objects were passed through the large hole, into the waiting hands of the men standing outside.

Anger churned up the bile inside Officer Namsky's stomach. He wanted to arrest the entire crowd, but he knew that he couldn't . He had to stay by the door and protect the narcotics inside the drugstore. His mouth was very dry and he found it hard to swallow. It felt as though he were trying to swallow a large ball of cotton.

A young man in the group, who was watching Ted Namsky, picked up a large rock and threw it at the top of the already cracked window. A large hunk of glass fell out. An agonizing scream filled the night air. Ted didn't have to see to know what had happened. That piece of falling glass had found a victim!

The hell with the property, thought Ted. A human life was more important than anything else! He made a mad-dash for the novelty store.

When Ted left his post, he could see the small group of men making their move also. A young boy, approximately fifteen-years-old, laid on the floor of the novelty store. His right leg had been amputated from the knee cap down. Crimson colored liquid covered the entire floor around him. The young boy shrieked in agony.

The crowd stood still. No one tried to help the bleeding boy. Ted crawled into the store through the hole in the window. He removed his baton from his belt and picked up a heavy rubber balloon from the floor. Tying the balloon around the youth's leg, Ted slipped the baton in between the balloon and the boy's thigh. He slowly began twisting the baton in a circular motion. The balloon tightened around the boy's thigh, eventually stopping the bleeding.

Ted quickly looked around at the crowd, shouting, "Someone come in here and give me a hand with this kid!" An old man crept into the store through the open hole.

"Hold this baton and don't release it!" Ted ordered. "I'm going over to my car to call for an ambulance."

The old man shook his head in approval as he took hold of the baton and held onto it - tightly. Ted left the novelty store and ran to the squad car. The open back door to the drugstore caught his eye. Ted entered the squad car and requested the dispatcher to send a squadrol or an ambulance for the injured boy.

After delivering his message, Ted exited the squad car and ran over to the drugstore's rear exit door. He peeked into the store. From what he could see, there were approximately twelve people running around inside. They were helping themselves , knocking objects off shelves, breaking showcases, stuffing items into their pockets and drinking the whiskey they had taken off the shelves. The looters laughed, talked and cheered at their good fortune.

Ted saw a man heading for the doorway where he was standing. His arms were filled with various items - coffee pots, toasters, irons and bottles of whiskey.

Officer Namsky flattened his body against the brick building. He reached for his baton, but it was gone. He reached into his back pocket, took out his 'sap' (blackjack) and waited for the man. When instinct told him that the looter was just about even with the end of the doorjamb, Ted swung his sap, at eye level, towards the middle of the doorjamb. He had judged right. The sap had found its target. Teeth and blood fell to the sidewalk, followed by a loud agonizing scream. Glass bottles hit the concrete and exploded with a fury. Other items bounced off the sidewalk and rolled towards the street.

The looter ran into the street, screaming in pain, while holding his mouth with both hands, trying to stop the bleeding and the pain. He darted across the street and disappeared into the shadows of a dark alley.

Ted stood against the brick building again and waited. He could hear the sound of footsteps approaching. Just as a man stepped out onto the sidewalk, Ted grabbed him by his shoulder, spun him around and slammed him against the building.

"Hold it, man! Hold it!"pleaded the looter. "I'm clean! See, my hands are empty. I just went inside to have a look around." The looter held his hands high in theair. Ted watched him closely, noticing that the man's sport shirt was too large for his body frame.

"What's under the shirt, my sneaky friend?"asked Ted, hitting his "Sap" against his hand.

"Hey! Believe me, man. I told you the truth. I'm clean. I ain't got nothin under my shirt." the looter insisted.

"Oh no?" We'll see about that." Officer Namsky whipped the sap in a quick-sweeping motion across the looter's midsection, lightly striking his abdomen in several different places. The sound of breaking glass accompanied each blow of the sap . The looter squeezed his eyes closed tightly, his face revealing a surprised, anguished expression. "Oh no, man!" he shouted. "Oh Lordy, no!"

The front of the looter's shirt and pants changed colors as they became soaked from the liquid substance. The odor of alcohol was so strong that Officer Namsky had to back away before the smell overtook him. The looter opened his eyes slowly.

"You ain't gonna arrest me now, Officer?" the looter pleaded. "Not after what you just did to me."

"Just stay right where you are!"ordered Ted as he sat down in the squad car. He picked up the microphone and waited for the dispatcher to clear the line.

"Attention all cars!"announced the dispatcher. "The situation has become critical! There are no squadrols available to transport prisoners to the district stations. They're transporting injured persons to the hospitals. If you have a major felon in custody, transport him to the station, per your own vehicle. Do not make misdemeanor arrests. If you find merchandise in the streets, place it back into the stores."

Ted replaced the microphone in its holder. What the hell's the sense of calling? he thought. I can't get any help and I can't leave here. Ted exited the squad car and walked over to the looter.

"You gonna cut me loose, man?" the looter pleaded again. "Are you going to let me go?"

"Sure, man."Ted smiled. "I'm gonna cut you loose."

"Great, man! That's great!"shouted the looter, starting to take his pants off.

"Whoa! What the hell are you doing?" Ted asked.

"I'm taking off my pants, man. I gotta get rid of all this glass inside my pants!"

"Oh-no-no-no!" Ted interrupted, waving his hands in disapproval. "You can't take your pants off out here in the street. There are too many women and children walking around. Besides, if you did, I'd have to arrest you for indecent exposure. No, just leave your pants on."

"Hey, man,"cried the looter,"I can't make a single move without cutting myself. Please! Let me get rid of all this glass!" he pleaded again.

"Yes , I see that we do have a problem, don't we?" said Ted. "We can't have you dumping all of that glass out on the public way. Who knows, some child may fall and cut their self. Tell you what we'll do, my friend. Since all of that glass belongs to you, I'll let you take it all home with you and you can dump it into your own garbage can. How far do you live from here?

"Two blocks, sir," answered the looter, " but-------"

"Two blocks isn't too far," interrupted Ted. "Now this is what you'll do. Take your pant cuffs and tuck them into your socks. That way, when you run home, you won't spill any of that dangerous, sharp glass all over the sidewalk."

"Run?"screamed the looter. "Hell, man, I'm afraid to move, let alone - run!"

"Do what you're told!"ordered Officer Namsky, in a stern voice. The looter tucked his pant cuffs into his socks.

"Now - run!" Ted shouted.

The looter began walking slowly, letting out *Oh's* and *Aw's* with each step he took.

"The next time you decide to loot a store, you'll think twice about it." Ted raised his hand. "Now run, you son-of-a-bitch! Run!"

Ted swung his sap across the looter's buttocks. The looter screamed in pain and began a slow, jerking running stride down the street.

What the hell is Tony doing at the front entrance? thought Ted. Why did he let all of those people inside the store? Ted walked towards the front of the drugstore. He saw the problem. A group of people had backed Tony up against a brick wall and were shouting obscenities at him, keeping his view away from the front door.

Only one way to handle this, thought Ted. He removed his revolver from his holster. Got to get those people out of this drugstore. He entered the store through the rear door.

"All right, all you Goddamn looters," he shouted, "drop everything you've taken and line up against that wall!"

"You is just bluffin', man!"shouted a male looter, laughing as he picked up more merchandise. "You isn't gonna shoot no one."

Ted squeezed the trigger on his revolver and fired two shots into the ceiling. Everyone stood motionless. The heckler continued, "Hell, man, two shots in the ceiling ain't gonna scare anyone! I wants what I wants and what I wants - I takes!"

Ted leveled his revolver and fired two more rounds. This time, the lead bullets flew six inches above the looter's head. Two clocks fell off a wall and shattered as they hit the floor. The heckler screamed and dropped everything that he was holding.

"You crazy, man! Crazy!" he screamed. The looter turned and threw a case of beer bottles through the large plate glass window. Everyone in the store made a mad dash for the gaping hole in the window. Ted let them run. Everything had been left in the store: besides, they hadn't gotten into the narcotics cabinet - yet.

The crowd outside heard the shots and ran away with those who had been inside the drugstore. Tony walked over to the hole in the window.

"You O.K., Ted?" he asked, hoping he would hear an answer.

"Yeah, I'm O.K., Tony. Get your ass inside the store. We'll have to stay inside and stand guard until someone gets here to relieve us.

Ted and Tony watched as the crowd outside overturned their squad car in the middle of the street and cheered as they set it afire...

CHAPTER XXIII

It felt great to work the day watch again. The riots had long passed. The hot rays of the bright sun felt good against Ted's face. He was glad it was summer again.

Leon drove the squad car as Ted took in the beauty of the scenery. Officers Barner and Seccoro were on their regular days off.

"Nothing like the good old summertime, huh, Ted?" laughed Leon.

Ted smiled and closed his eyes. "Nothing like it, buddy," he answered, lazily. "Nothing like it."

Leon hit the brakes, bringing the squad car to a screeching halt, almost sending Ted through the windshield.

"What the hell are you trying to do, kill me?" Ted yelled, squeezing his right elbow that was in pain.

"Look over there!" Leon shouted, pointing towards a three story brick apartment building. An elderly woman stood in the middle of the street screaming hysterically. Smoke, followed by large engulfing flames, poured out the second floor windows of the apartment building.

"Holy Mother in Heaven!" exclaimed Ted. "Get over there quick , Leon!" Ted grabbed the microphone.

"Emergency! Emergency!" he shouted.

"All cars stand by," responded the dispatcher. "Go ahead - with the emergency!"

"This is Car 1246. We've got a three story apartment building burning at Clyborn and Halsted. Better get some squad cars and fire equipment over here in a hurry! It's gonna be a hell of a blaze from the looks of it!" said Ted.

"Ten-four, 1246," said the dispatcher.

Ted and Leon quickly exited their squad car and ran to the screaming woman. They took hold of her arms and tried to calm her down so they could talk with her, but she was speaking Spanish. The woman repeated the phrase "Mio nina" over and over, staring wild eyed at the burning building.

"What's she trying to say?" asked Ted, hampered by the language barrier.

"Beats me?" answered Leon. "Hold onto her while I go through the crowd and find someone who can translate for us."

Leon came back a moment later with an elderly man following close behind him. The woman kept repeating the same phrase over and over again.

"What's she saying?" Ted asked the old man.

"She keeps saying - *My girl! My girl!* I think she's trying to tell us that her little daughter is inside of that burning building."

"Good God!"exclaimed Officer Bukowski, looking at the burning inferno.

"Hold onto the woman, Leon."Ted shouted. He ran towards the burning building.

"Where the hell you going, Ted?" Leon yelled.

Ted ignored his partner. He ran through the entrance door leading into the building. "Little girl! Hey, Little girl!" He shouted. "Where are you? Don't be afraid! Just yell out so I'll know where you're at."

The hallway on the first floor began filling up with a thick, black, choking smoke. Ted's eyes burned badly. He took out his handkerchief and covered his face, then quickly darted up the hallway stairs.

The second floor hallway of the building was filled with smoke. The flames were leaping up the sides of the wall.

She couldn't be on this floor, thought Ted. If she were, she'd already be dead from the heat and the thick smoke. The flames quickly ate their way up the stairway, chomping at the aged wooden floor boards. The strong smell of gasoline filled Ted's nostrils. He decided to take a wild chance and hoped that he was right. He dashed up the stairway to the third floor - two steps at a time.

"Hey! Little girl! Where are you?" he shouted.

Ted listened for some kind of reply, but all he could hear was the sound of the crackling, burning wood. Suddenly, he heard the soft whimpering of a child's voice. Frantically, Ted searched each apartment on the floor. In the last apartment, at the far end of the hallway, he hit pay dirt.

Kicking open the door, he spotted a small child huddled in a corner of the room, clutching a doll. The child was too frightened to move. Ted rushed into the room and picked up the little girl in his arms. She dropped her doll as she hugged him tightly. He bent down, picked up her doll and handed it to her. His elbow ached from the blow it had received on the car dashboard, when Leon had stopped quickly. Ted forced the thought of the pain from his mind, trying to think only of escape from the burning building. The little girl continued to cry and hug Ted tightly.

"Don't be scared, honey," said Ted, trying to comfort her. "We'll get out of here."

Ted ran out of the apartment, still carrying the child. He ran down the hallway, only to be stopped when he reached the burning stairs. It was impossible to make their escape down the stairway. The staircase was a towering inferno, completely engulfed in flames! Ted searched for a way up to the roof, but the only door that led to the roof was nailed shut.

He ran back to the apartment where he had found the child. Slamming the door shut, he jammed a rug in the crack at the bottom of the door, hoping to keep some of the smoke out of the room for a little while. He could feel the heat on the bottom of his feet.

That could only mean one thing, thought Ted. The entire second floor was ablaze with fire! It wouldn't be long before the flames found their way to the apartment they were in. Ted had to get to the roof. At least up there, they would stand a chance of escaping when the Fire Department arrived.

Ted pulled open the living room window and looked down into the street. At least a hundred people had gathered to watch the fire. A twelve-inch brick ledge, below the window sill, surrounded the entire building. Approximately ten feet from the apartment window, a small metal ladder was anchored to the building. It lead to the roof.

The glowing, eager flames crept upward. The fire was now only four feet below the concrete ledge. Suddenly, Ted heard a loud cracking noise. He tightly held onto the little girl and made his way out onto the concrete ledge.

The living room floor suddenly caved in at the center of the room. The bright red, hungry flames leaped up towards the ceiling.

"Just hold me tight, sweetheart, and don't let go, no matter what happens!" Ted whispered into the child's ear.

She held onto his neck as tightly as she could. Ted slowly slid his feet across the concrete ledge, heading directly for the metal ladder. His feet burned from the heat below him. He could see the approaching fire engines, just a few blocks away.

Suddenly, the concrete ledge, where he was standing, broke away from the building. Ted tried to catch his balance, but finally fell backwards. Clutching the child tightly against his chest, Ted closed his eyes and prayed, as they both fell towards the rushing sidewalk below.

Several hours later, Ted finally regained consciousness. For a moment, he didn't know where he was at, then the surroundings around him made him realize that he was in a hospital. Leon sat in a chair, next to Ted's bed.

"How's the hero?" Leon asked, smiling and poking Ted's arm.

"Feeling poorly and sore, but lucky to be alive - I guess? How's the little girl?" he asked, very concerned.

"She's doing fine, Ted, thanks to the hero! Your body broke the fall for her. She only sustained a broken knee cap and received some cuts and bruises. She'll be fine in a couple of months."

"That's some good news," Ted said, trying to shift his body to another position. Suddenly, he realized that his body was *numb* from the waist down!

"Leon!" he shouted, almost becoming hysterical. "I can't move my legs! I can't feel them! What's wrong with me?"

"Take it easy, pal," Leon interrupted, trying to comfort his partner. "You landed on a pile of soft dirt. That's what saved you both. Unfortunately, you injured your spine, but the doctors sat that, in time, you'll be your old self again."

Ted's body went limp from exhaustion because of his efforts to move his legs.

CHAPTER XXIV

The beginning of September came upon them. Ted maneuvered his wheelchair over to his living room window. The weather had already begun to get cool with the setting of the sun. A breeze came in through the open window. Ted felt a slight chill run through his body. He grabbed a sweater from the table next to him and put it around his shoulders. He was very despondent. He had visited with the little girl several times while they were in the hospital together. She recovered very rapidly and soon went to their new home. Ted had promised to visit her just as soon as he could get around on his own.

It had been several weeks since his friends had been over to visit him. Ted slowly rubbed his hand back and forth over the rubber wheel on his wheelchair. He watched two small birds search for food on the small lawn in front of his house. Looking at the street, he remembered those happy days when Tracy would pick him up for work. He could still visualize her standing at the curb, next to her car, smiling and waving to him - in her own little special way.

He let his head hang forward. Tears slowly filled his eyes. And where were his friends? Was he forgotten already? "Why did you have to die, Tracy?" he whispered. He didn't pay any attention to the blue and white squad car that stopped in front of his house. He had turned and wheeled himself away from the window.

Sergeant Conley, along with Officers Barner, Bukowski and Tony Seccoro, got out of the squad car. They walked up to the front door of the rooming house. Sergeant Conley rang the doorbell and waited. An elderly woman, dressed in an old blue house dress, opened the door.

"How's Ted doing, Mrs. Simpson?" asked the sergeant.

"Not too good, Sergeant," the woman answered, sadly. "He just sits in that wheelchair and stares out the window. He never leaves his room. I usually bring him his meals. He refuses any kind of help."

"We've got to do something to cheer him up,"Tony interrupted, holding up a small package.

"Go right up stairs, Officers, " replied Mrs. Simpson. "I'd like to see a little happiness in his face."

Sergeant Conley tipped his hat as he passed the woman. "Thanks, Mrs. Simpson, " he answered. "We'll try."

The four officers stopped outside the door to Ted's room. Sergeant Conley knocked softly.

"I don't need anything, Mrs. Simpson!" Ted shouted, startled by the knock.

"It's Sergeant Conley and a couple of the guys from the station to see you, Ted," said the sergeant. "Is it all right if we come in?" he asked.

"Sure, come on in!" Ted replied, eager to see who was with the sergeant.

Sergeant Conley opened the door. The sight of his four friends standing in the doorway brought a quick smile to Ted's face.

"High-ya-doin', buddy," said Leon Bukowski.

"Not too bad, "Ted answered, sadly. "Sit down and make yourselves comfortable."

Sergeant Conley instantly caught the sadness and loneliness in Ted's voice when he spoke. The sergeant sat down and made himself at home. "By the way, Ted, that little girl you saved is doing great. She got rid of the cast on her leg yesterday and she's walking around as good as ever."

Ted looked down and stared at his wheelchair. "That's great, Sarge. Just great." he answered.

Leon interrupted the conversation. Walking over to Ted, he placed his hand on Ted's shoulder. "Don't worry, Ted, in a few more weeks you'll be walking, too. It's just going to take you a little longer. Don't worry, buddy, you'll make out all right."

"Make out all right? What the hell do you know. A few weeks after the accident, I thought that I was getting some feeling back into my legs. Believe me, I really thought I was! The doctor checked me over and said the prognosis looked good. He said that I could be walking again in several months after taking therapy. I tried! The feeling was there! But, I just couldn't make those legs move." shouted Ted. He slammed his hand angrily against the arm rest on his wheelchair. He continued. " I got a visit from the Doc today. He brought me some really great news."

Ted wheeled himself over to a small desk, opened the middle drawer and took out two white envelopes. He handed them to Leon . "Read these aloud, Leon, so that everyone can hear you," he said.

Officer Burkowski looked at the return address on one envelope. It was the hospital's address. Leon removed the sheet of paper from the envelope. He silently read the letter for a few moments, then slowly began reading aloud:

>   Mr. Ted Namsky:
>   After careful examination of all tests taken of your
>   injuries, it is in my opinion, as well as my colleagues,

that the injuries are permanent and that the chances of you walking again are very unlikely.

Dr. James Tuttle

Leon was stunned at what he had just read. He slowly folded the letter and placed it back into the envelope.

Doesn't that frost your balls,Leon?"said Ted. "Those son- of-a-bitches were just humoring me. They didn't want my mind to go into a state of depression if I knew that I was never going to walk again. They gave me that letter to give to the pension board."

" Aw, don't worry, Ted, we'll take you to see some other doctors for a second - third - and even a fourth opinion if we have too. We're not giving up!" said Leon, feeling a lump starting to form inside his throat.

"Leon, I called the pension board and told them what the doctor had told me. They asked me for the letter, which I had a copy made and sent to them. Read the second letter, Leon. That's the letter that the pension board sent to me," said Ted.

Leon looked at the return address of the second envelope. It was from the Police Pension Board.

"What did they say, Ted?" asked Sergeant Conley.

""Read it aloud, Leon!" Ted shouted as he maneuvered his wheelchair over to the open window. He stared down at the street as Leon removed the sheet of paper from the envelope. He read aloud again:

Officer Ted Namsky:

After receiving your letter and confirming with your attending physicians about your injuries, we are informed that your injuries are permanent and that you are unable to perform your normal duties as a police officer. Therefore, it is the unanimous decision of our Board of Review, that as of the above listed date, you are to be put on a permanent disability pension.

Leon couldn't finish reading the rest of the letter. He laid it down on the desk. The four officers stared at Ted - everyone remaining silent. Tony looked at his hands and suddenly realized he was carrying a package for Ted. He walked over to the wheelchair. "Ted," he began, "all the guys on the watch chipped in and we got a present for you." He placed the package in Ted's lap

Ted picked up the package and read the attached card. He slipped the ribbon off the box, then ripped the wrapping paper covering it. The gift consisted of two items - a brand new short-wave portable radio and a police scanner radio that received the local police calls.

"The fellas thought you might like to listen to what is going on in the district while you are temporarily laid up," said Sergeant Conley.

Ted slowly turned his wheelchair around until he faced the four officers. A tiny trickle of water fell from the corner of his eye. "Tell-----," Ted hesitated a moment. "Tell them all that I really appreciate these gifts."

"Let me set them up for you, Ted," volunteered Tony, picking up the units from Ted's lap. He fumbled with the tiny crystal that would locate the right frequency for their district.

"There you go, Ted," said Tony, proud of his achievement. The police dispatcher blurted out several orders for squad cars.

Ted reached over and turned off the radio. "I don't feel much like listening to the calls right now, fellas," he replied.

"Sure, we understand." said Leon, anxious to leave the room for fear of his old partner seeing him beginning to cry. "We've really got to be going, Ted. We'll drop by again later on in the week to see how you're getting along."

"Sure - sure fellas, I understand." said Ted, showing a forced smile.

The officers said their good-byes and began leaving the room. Officer Bukowski was the last one to leave. "Leon!" Officer Bukowski turned around. "Yeah, buddy," he replied.

"Be careful, Leon," Ted continued. "Don't wind up like me, confined to a Goddamn wheelchair!"

Leon gave his friend a short salute. "I won't, Ted. I won't!" he said, as he left the room and shut the door behind him.

The other officers waited for Leon at the far end of the hallway.

"Is he in a better mood, now that we've gone?" asked Sergeant Conley.

"No, he's in a bad way, Sarge!" said Leon. "His moral just hit bottom."

"Aw, he'll snap out of it," interrupted Tony. "Time, patience, understanding and a lot more therapy will bring him back to his senses." They started down the stairway.

Ted wheeled himself over to the closet, opened the door and removed his service revolver from the holster. Placing the gun in his lap, he wheeled himself back to the open window. He switched on the radio scanner and turned up the volume as loud as it would go.

The four officers had just reached the middle of the front sidewalk, when they heard the blare of police calls coming from Ted's room.

"See," said Tony, reassuringly. "I told you he'd snap out of his depression. He's listening to his new radio already."

Suddenly, the crack of gunfire came from Ted's room! The loud explosion echoed through Leon Bukowski's head like a hundred cannons going off at one time.

Sergeant Conley, Tim Barner and Tony Seccoro ran back into the rooming house. Leon, feeling totally helpless, stood still, staring up at his friend's open window. A small wisp of blue smoke found its way out through the window.

Leon couldn't go back into the room. He knew what he'd find when he got there. He wanted to remember his friend as he had been when he had first met Ted - full of humor and life!

Sergeant Conley stuck his head out of the open window and shouted down to Leon, "Call for a squadrol, Leon! Ted's gone!"

Leon slowly walked back to the squad car and sat down. Tears flowed freely from both his eyes as he picked up the microphone. Another squad car had pulled up across the street. Leon looked at the slogan on the blue and white's door and said it aloud, "**TO SERVE AND PROTECT!** We're the *First Line Defense* for the public. They despise us when we're not needed and screamed at when we don't arrive fast enough when they need us."

"Life sucks!" he shouted. "**YOU SERVE! YOU PROTECT!** And then **YOU DIE!**

Leon notified the dispatcher, then waited for the squadrol that would transport him and his old partner, together - for the very last time!